Chase's voice was sharp as a knife

"Listen," he said coldly, "listen and get this straight. You're an intruder—a trespasser. Heaven knows what you did to Billy so you could take his place, but the fact is you're not wanted."

"Isn't that too bad?" Nicole said, more calmly than she felt.

Chase's mouth twisted. "Damned right, it is. Putting you ashore will mean I've lost the race. I could never make up the time."

Was it really that simple, Nicole thought, in elation. All the time she'd wondered how to sabotage his boat—she was the disabling factor. Tarrant would be out of the race the minute he made for land.

"Which is why I'm not going to do it," Chase went on softly, chillingly. "I'm not going to put you ashore."

SANDRA MARTON says she's always believed in romance. She wrote her first love story when she was nine and fell madly in love at sixteen with the man who is her husband. Today they live on Long Island, midway between the glitter of Manhattan and the quiet beaches of the Atlantic. Sandra is delighted to be writing the kinds of stories she loves and even happier to find that her readers enjoy them, too.

Books by Sandra Marton

SANDRA MARTON

eye of the storm

Harlequin Books

TORONTO • NEW YORK • LONDON
AMSTERDAM • PARIS • SYDNEY • HAMBURG
STOCKHOLM • ATHENS • TOKYO • MILAN

Harlequin Presents first edition February 1990
ISBN 0-373-11244-0

Original hardcover edition published in 1989
by Mills & Boon Limited

CHAPTER ONE

NICOLE WHEELER stood on the sandy Florida beach, her hazel eyes narrowed against the glare of the sun on the turquoise water of the Atlantic. It was the kind of January morning that made it hard to remember the mid-western winters she'd left only a year ago.

She brushed back a strand of chestnut hair, then took a few steps forward until she stood ankle-deep in the water, closing her eyes with pleasure as a gust of wind blew across her sweat-dampened skin. Hot sun, cool water, warm breezes—a perfect day for Aston to teach her to sail the little boat that lay beside her, its stern in the water.

A sleek powerboat gunned past, dark and swift as a shark. Nicole curled her toes into the sand as the boat's wake rocked the gentle play of surf against shore. The sailing-boat rocked, too, and she bent and touched a steadying hand to the hull.

'Easy,' she whispered, as if the boat were a highly-strung racehorse that needed gentling.

Nicole straightened and looked towards the water again. The powerboat was racing up the channel, heading for the open sea. She could see the man at the wheel. He was naked from the waist up, his shoulders broad and powerful. His long body lounged back in the leather seat with a casual insolence. There was something aggressive about him and his boat, something she found disconcerting, even as her eyes followed him.

'Nicki?'

She blinked and looked over her shoulder. Aston Powell

was trudging through the white sand towards her. She smiled, but her smile faded when she realised how he was dressed. You didn't sail a Sunfish in a suit and tie.

'We're not taking the boat out?' she asked when he reached her.

Aston put his arm lightly around her shoulders and his handsome face creased in an apologetic smile. 'I'm terribly sorry. I know we had a date, but something's come up.'

Nicole tilted her head to the side. 'Don't tell me,' she said lightly. 'There's some kind of crisis about the Mystery Boat.'

His smile flickered. 'Not a crisis, exactly. Just a question about sails. I have to drive to Palm Beach and . . .'

Nicole laughed softly. 'Honestly, Aston, you spend more time with that sailing-boat than you ever spend at the office.'

For a second, his smile seemed to harden around the edges, but then the corners of his mouth relaxed and it curved across his face again.

'Is that my private secretary speaking, Miss Wheeler, or the woman I'm going to marry?'

A flush rose on Nicole's cheeks and she moved free of his encircling arm. 'Aston,' she said quickly, 'I haven't promised anything. I only said I'd . . .'

'I know what you said, Nicki—that you'd think about our future.' He put his hand beneath her chin and lifted her face to his. 'But you can't blame me for trying.'

He was always trying, Nicole thought as she looked into his pale eyes. He'd been trying ever since she'd gone to work as his private secretary after moving to Coral City. First he'd tried to date her, then to make the relationship intimate. To her surprise, her refusal had only changed his goal. He'd gone from asking her to go home with him to asking her to marry him. And last night, after weeks of refusals, she'd finally agreed to consider the future.

'. . . if I get back early enough. How's that sound?'

Nicole blinked her eyes. 'I'm sorry, I was daydreaming, Aston. Did you ask me something?'

'I said, why don't you spend the morning here? Take a swim, have lunch at the clubhouse—I don't expect to be gone all day. I'll stop by and pick you up and we'll drive down to that little place in the Keys for dinner.'

She smiled at him. 'If it's early enough, you could still show me how to handle the Sunfish.'

He grinned. 'It's a deal. It won't take you any time to learn to sail it, Nicki. This is just a small version of *Fortune's Fancy*.'

Nicole laughed. '*Fortune's Fancy* is a thirty-nine-foot sloop, Aston.'

'Well, you got the hang of it quickly enough, didn't you?' He hugged her against his side. 'You're the best crew my sloop ever had.'

Nicole tossed her head. 'But not good enough to crew the Mystery Boat in the Coral City to Barbados Race, hmm?'

'No,' he said sharply, 'you're not.' She stared at him in surprise, and he gave a quick little laugh. 'Sorry, sweetheart. I didn't mean to bite your head off. But you know what I mean—I need someone with more experience. Until I taught you to sail, you'd never been out on anything bigger than a rowing-boat on Lake Michigan. You said so yourself.'

'I was teasing, Aston,' Nicole said softly. 'Of course I understand.'

'I just want to win this damned race,' he said. 'That's all.'

She nodded. 'I know.'

He smiled and drew her towards him. Nicole put her face up for his kiss, drawing back as she always did before he could deepen it. She waved to him as he hurried away, and then she walked down to the shore again and sank down beside the Sunfish.

She really would have to stop teasing Aston, she thought as she stretched her legs out in the cool water. The race, and the boat he'd commissioned, were taboo, that was all. He didn't have any sense of humour where either was concerned.

Nicole had never seen him this determined about anything, certainly not about the Powell Corporation. Aston ran it with a casual ease that should have put a dent in the firm's balance sheets. But contracts seemed to fall into his lap. The land development company never lacked for new business.

'The Powell charm,' Aston said whenever the firm won a new project. And then he'd smile that charmingly boyish smile of his. 'I'm not a hard-driving dynamo, Nicki. But you're not going to hold that against me, are you?'

Nicole sighed as she leaned back on her elbows and looked out to sea. How could she hold it against him? She'd barely survived a marriage in which success was a god to be worshipped at all costs, a god to whom love was readily sacrificed. Tony had taught her that men who were driven by the need to win were men to whom relationships were expendable.

The result was that she rather liked Aston's casual attitude towards business. As for his near-obsession with winning the sailing race—well, that had puzzled her at first, but then she'd understood it. Racing got into the blood quickly—hadn't she bragged for weeks after they'd come in first in the club's regatta?

She sat up, drew her legs in, and looped her arms around her knees. The only thing she didn't understand was why she couldn't make a commitment to Aston Powell. She wasn't in love with him, but she wasn't a foolish child any more. She wasn't looking for love, not the heart-stopping, story-book kind. She'd had that once, and look where it had got her.

Aston offered everything a woman could want. He was good-looking, he was wealthy—and he was pressuring her for a commitment. It was a subtle pressure but it was there, and sometimes it was discomfiting. Nicole had learned never to admire anything in a shop window— it would turn up on her desk the next day. She suspected that even the Sunfish had been bought because of an innocent remark the past week.

She and Aston had been watching boardboats race. 'Those look like fun,' she'd said.

The very next day, Aston had purchased the Sunfish. 'I thought you'd like to try it, Nicki.'

Nicole's delight in the little boat had been tempered by something in his voice. 'I hope you didn't buy this just for me,' she'd said.

Something that was not quite a smile had twisted across Aston's mouth. 'I'd buy you the sun and the moon if you'd let me, Nicki.'

His eyes met hers, and she knew he was remembering all the expensive gifts she'd refused in the past months. Finally, he'd shrugged. 'I always wanted a Sunfish. I just never got around to it, that's all.' Nicole sighed. She hadn't argued: if the boat was a gift, at least it was an impersonal one. And now here she was, on a beautiful morning, sitting beside the Sunfish instead of sailing it . . .

'Miss Wheeler?'

She looked up. Jimmy, one of the boys who worked at the marina, was standing beside her.

'Hi, Jimmy,' she said, smiling at him. 'What can I do for you?'

'Mr Powell sent me. He told me to put the Sunfish back on the rack.'

Nicole made a face and got to her feet. 'Yes, I guess you'd better. We were going to take it out, but something came up.'

The boy nodded. 'I guess you were really looking forward to it, huh? I mean, the breeze is gonna be steady all day.'

'Yes,' she admitted, touching the sleek hull lightly, 'I was. Mr Powell was going to teach me to sail this morning.'

Jimmy cocked his head. 'Teach you? Heck, Miss Wheeler, he don't need to teach you. I've seen you on *Fortune's Fancy* plenty of times. You can sail.'

'Yes, but not a Sunfish. It's different, isn't it?'

The boy shrugged. 'Nah, not really. If you can sail, you can sail. That's all there is to it.

Nicole smiled. 'I'll bet.'

'No, I mean it. Why, I could show you all you gotta know in a few minutes.' The boy grinned. 'Look over there.'

She swung towards the ocean, her hazel eyes following his pointing finger. A boat the duplicate of the Sunfish was fairly flying across the water. The girl sailing it looked younger than Jimmy, and she clearly having a wonderful time.

'See?' Jimmy said. 'There's nothing to it.'

Nicole caught her lower lip between her teeth. She *could* sail, that was the truth. Even Aston said she'd caught on fast. What could possibly happen if she took the boat out? She could end up in the water—well, so what? She wasn't afraid of getting wet. In fact, with the temperature rising, getting wet was something to look forward to.

She shaded her eyes with her hand. There were two small boardboats on the water now, and their occupants were yelling challenges at each other. Both hulls dug in as a gust of wind ballooned their sails. The first boat heeled too far and its helmsman toppled into the water. The girl came up laughing, grasped the hull and clambered back on board.

'They never sink,' Jimmy said. 'See? That kid's getting right back on.'

That kid. Nicole took a deep breath. 'OK, Jimmy,' she said, 'you talked me into it. She punched the boy's arm lightly and grinned. 'Just tell me what I have to do.'

The boy smiled. 'Sure thing, Miss Wheeler. You'll see, you're gonna have a great time.'

A while later, out alone in the Sunfish with the wind filling the boat's gaily striped sail. Nicole laughed aloud. She'd have to remember to tell Jimmy he'd been absolutely, positively right. This was wonderful! *Fortune's Fancy* was fun, but this—*this* was sailing! The slightest weight-shift, the simplest pressure on the tiller, and the boat responded instantly.

Jimmy's last shouted advice had been to stay close to shore. 'Just until you get the feel of things, you know? To be on the safe side.'

Nicole did just that—it seemed sensible. But, as the morning wore on, her confidence grew. There was an island at the head of the harbour, a palmetto-covered mound of rock thrusting up from the water with what seemed to be the ruins of a Victorian mansion tucked deep within the trees. She'd seen it lots of times from Aston's sloop as they'd sailed up the channel to the open sea. And she'd always wanted to explore it.

Why not? She shoved the tiller to starboard. The wind had picked up, which made sailing a little more arduous than it had been at first. Not that she minded: she liked the speed, the sensation of skimming over the water in a wash of foam.

The boat was heeling sharply and Nicole, perched on the gunwale, planted her feet firmly in the shallow well and leaned back until her upper body was over the water. Hiking out, it was called: using your weight to counterbalance the wind's push on the sail. It made her feel as if she and the swift-moving boat were one.

The Sunfish was flying, its hull so sharply angled that the world tilted crazily. Not that she could see terribly much of it: between the wind-filled sail, the boat's speed and her own excitement, it was hard to keep a clear view. The island had to be coming up soon, though. Maybe, she thought, maybe it was time to slow down.

All she had to do was ease the main sheet. She grinned as she thought of how pleased Aston would be when she told him she'd finally started to think of the rope that controlled the sail as a sheet, although why it was called that . . .

Her smile faded. The sheet wouldn't move. She tugged hard, grunting with effort, but it wouldn't give an inch. It had to be caught on something It . . . yes, there it was. The rope had jammed in the pulley

'Come on,' she muttered, and she bent towards the rope and pulled at it furiously. It didn't move, but the Sunfish did, responding instantly to the sudden shift of her weight. The hull tilted alarmingly, and Nicole quickly leaned backwards again.

'Keep her balanced, Miss Wheeler. If you don't, she'll go over.'

Jimmy's voice seemed to echo in her ears. OK, she thought, OK, I won't bend down. I'll keep tugging and pulling and . . .

'Damn!' Her breath hissed between her teeth. Nothing she did would free the stupid rope.

Think. Think. There had to be another way to slow the Sunfish. Yes, of course there was. What was the matter with her? All she had to do was turn into the wind. The sail would shake, the wind's power would be lost, and the boat would stop. You just had to shove the tiller over and . . .

No. This was impossible. The tiller wouldn't move,

either. It couldn't. Somehow, while she'd been struggling with the damned pulley, the rest of the line, the long length that lay in the shallow cockpit, had managed to snag the rudder, and now it was jammed tighter than a miser's purse.

Nicole's heart began to race. The boat was out of control, racing over the water like a creature escaping from hell.

The deep blast of a horn shattered the silence. The wind whipped her hair into her face as she twisted on her precarious perch and looked behind her. An enormous powerboat was coming up quickly, overtaking her with menacing speed, its bow slicing through the water and throwing a huge wave back along its sleek black sides. The growl of its engines carried clearly over the sounds of the straining sail and the pounding waves. The horn sounded again, three loud, jarring blasts, and Nicole felt them curl into the very marrow her bones.

'You damned fool!' she yelled. 'What the hell are you doing?'

Desperately, she tugged at the jammed rope and then smashed her hand against the tiller bar. 'Move!' she cried. 'Move, move . . .'

The horn blasted again. 'I can't get out of your way,' she screamed. 'Don't you understand?'

The wind whipped her words back into her face., Whoever was at the wheel of the powerboat couldn't possibly hear her—she knew that—but he could see her, damn him! Why didn't he veer away? He was going to run her down, run her down into the sea . . .

Her chest heaved in terror. What kind of crazy man was trying to kill her? He must know he was . . .

The growl of the engines deepened, became a snarl. The black hull loomed behind her, white foam cascading from its bow like saliva from the jaws of a rabid dog. Nicole threw up her arms and screamed, a long, thin sound that was lost in the roar of her pursuer's engines. Then, at the last possible second, the black boat skidded sharply and sliced across the Sunfish's wake. She screamed again as a wall of water roared towards her.

The wave hit the Sunfish a vicious blow. There was a sudden, stomach-wrenching lurch as the boat was lifted. Then, with a spill of sail, it tilted on its side and capsized. Nicole gasped a mouthful of air, and then the silent sea and the heavy weight of the sail settled over her.

She struck for the surface. But the rope wasn't finished with her yet. It had twisted around her legs, like a serpent intent on keeping its victim.

Oh, no! It was a silent scream, but it seemed to echo and re-echo in her mind. She was trapped, drowning beneath the warm tropical sea, a captive of the gaily striped sail and the sheet that was a rope . . .

No! She wouldn't die, not like this, not because some madman had chosen to ride her down. She would fight, she would free herself. She would . . .

Something brushed against her. Her eyes opened wide as a shape slid past her. It was a man, and something gleamed in his hand. He grabbed the ropes that held her and sawed at them, but they refused to part. Bubbles began to stream from her nose. Her lungs were bursting, burning, aching for air. In growing panic, she clutched at the man beside her. He pushed her hands away and slashed at the rope again. This time it parted and suddenly her legs were free.

Desperate for breath, Nicole lunged towards the surface. But the sail had become her shroud, holding her fast, drawing her towards that place from which there could be no return. Strong arms caught her, pulled her against a hard body. She had to breathe, didn't he understand? She fought silently, struggling against the iron-hard embrace, lashing out with her fists, kicking out with her feet. Finally— *finally*

—she kicked free.

Her head broke the surface and she gulped air into her lungs. She coughed as she swallowed a mouthful of water; her legs brushed against the sail and she flailed her arms in panic.

'Dammit, woman! Stop thrashing, do you hear me? Stop it, or I'll leave you here!'

The man's voice was hard and angry, but the threat brought her to her senses. She nodded weakly as he looped one arm around her and struck out towards the black boat lying still in the water with a powerful, one-handed stroke. She tried to grasp the boarding ladder when they reached it, but her muscles had turned to jelly. With a curse, the man caught her around the waist and shoved her upwards. She felt the rough clutch of his fingers at her hips, her buttocks, her thighs, and then she was tumbling over the side of the boat to fall in a wet, gasping huddle in the cockpit. She gagged and coughed up a mouthful of water just as he reached her side.

'Come on,' he said roughly, 'get up.'

Hands gripped her shoulders, hands that bruised her flesh as they pulled her to her feet. She coughed again, and he held her while she spat out another mouthful of salty liquid. Then she drew a breath deep into her lungs.

'I . . . I'm all right now, she gasped. 'Really . . .'

'What you are is a damned fool,' he snarled and, before she could answer, he lifted her into his arms.

'Please,' Nicole whispered, 'I'm fine. I . . .'

'If you are, it's none of your doing,' he said through his teeth.

His arms tightened around her with impersonal determination as he carried her down the ladder to the cabin below. She had a glimpse of dark wood and darker leather, and then he dumped her unceremoniously on a padded bench.

'Here,' he said brusquely. 'Put this on.' She looked up as

he thrust a white towelling robe at her. 'Well, go on. Put the damned thing on.'

Nicole stared at him. Reality was returning with a rush. Her rescuer was the reason she'd almost drowned. Did he think she was unware of that?

'I don't need your robe,' she said. 'If you'd help me right my boat . . .'

'You're going to go into shock if you're not careful. Get the robe on.'

'I am not going into shock. I . . .' But her teeth were beginning to chatter, even as she protested. He muttered something, bent and wrapped the robe around her shoulders. Nicole wanted to shrug it off; instead, she burrowed into its warmth. Her whole body had begun to tremble, and she'd never felt this cold in her life.

'Drink this.'

She looked up. He held a glass out to her, partly filled with an amber liquid.

'N—no,' she stammered, 'I d—d—don't . . .'

'It's brandy,' he said, and when she shook her head again he caught hold of her wrist and pulled her to her feet. 'Drink it,' he said grimly.

There was an edge to his voice that told her not to question the alternative. She took the glass from him, held it in both her hands, and lifted it to her lips.

'Every drop,' he warned.

The brandy was like liquid fire as it went down, but even before she'd finished it she could feel warmth spreading through her body.

'Better?' She nodded and he took the glass from her. 'OK. Now let me take a look at you.'

'I'm all right now,' she said. 'If you'd just . . .'

'Dammit, woman, must you argue about everything?' His hands closed on her shoulders and he forced her to turn towards him. 'I just want to see if you've any cuts or bruises.'

The brandy was working. She felt stronger, more in control. And, she thought, staring at the man who stood before her, a hell of a lot angrier.

'It's a little late to be so solicitous, isn't it? But, for your information, I'm fine now.'

'I'll be the judge of that,' he snapped, and before she could stop him his hands began moving lightly on her.

She stood still as his fingers probed beneath her hair. She felt them move across her scalp, down her neck, to her shoulders. He tilted her chin up, his touch impersonal, and she stared into his face, getting her first clear look at him.

Her first thought was that he was like his boat—dark and powerful. His hair, black as midnight, fell in thick, wet strands across his forehead and curled lightly on his neck. His skin was tanned, as if he spent all his time in the sun. Her eyes moved swiftly over a strong, straight nose to a firm mouth above a squared jaw. His shoulders were wide, his chest covered lightly with dark, curling hair in which drops of sea-water glistened. Her glance fell lower, to where a dark line of hair bisected his muscular abdomen and vanished beneath a brief black swimsuit.

'Do I meet with your approval?'

His voice was silky with amusement. Colour stained Nicole's cheeks as her eyes lifted to his, which were the palest grey she'd ever seen.

'Are you satisfied?' she asked coldly.

He laughed softly as his eyes moved slowly over her. 'Yeah, as much as I've seen.'

She slapped at his hand as he caught the lapel of the robe. 'You know what I meant,' she said stiffly. 'Except for the fact that I almost drowned, I'm fine.'

The corners of his mouth twitched. 'Don't you want me to double-check?'

Nicole lifted her chin. 'You damned near killed me.'

His eyebrows rose. 'Did I, now?'

'You know you did.' Her voice was cold. 'You ran me down.'

'I didn't run you down,' he said with exaggerated care. 'I dumped you.'

His words held a self-assured arrogance. She looked into his face, into those cold eyes, and then turned away. You didn't argue with a maniac, she told herself, certainly not one who boasted about almost having killed you.

'What the hell did you think you were doing, anyway?' His voice was rough with anger.

'What did it look like I was doing? I was sailing.'

'Really? You sure as hell could have fooled me.'

Nicole's eyes narrowed. 'I wouldn't expect you to understand anything about sailing.'

His eyebrows rose. 'Would you care to explain that remark, Miss . . .?'

'Wheeler,' she snapped. 'And I'd love to explain it. People like you . . .'

He tilted his head to the side. 'People like me?' he asked in a way that should have warned her to silence. But anger had loosened her tongue.

'Yes,' she said, 'that's right. You had a good time out there, blasting your horn, threatening me with your damned brute of a boat . . .'

She broke off as he smiled. His teeth gleamed whitely against his tanned face.

'Go on,' he said in a voice soft with malice. 'Let's hear the rest.'

'I'm surprised you're interested in what I have to say. Hell, you didn't think twice about me when you were running me down.'

He took a step towards her. 'Who taught you how to sail, Miss Wheeler?'

'That's none of your business.'

'Because whoever it is doesn't know a damned thing.'

Her chin lifted. 'That's not true. He's an excellent sailor.'

He smiled coldly. 'So is Popeye.'

Nicole tossed back her wet hair. 'You, of course, know all about sailing.'

'I sure as hell know more than whoever taught you.'

Her eyes darkened with anger. 'Whatever you are, mister, you're not a sailor. You're just a man with a macho toy . . .'

'Miss Wheeler——'

'I could have drowned, did you ever think of that?'

'Miss Wheeler, if you'd just listen for a moment . . .'

Nicole shook her head. 'No, *you* listen. If you're waiting for me to thank you for rescuing me, you're going to wait a long time. A very long time. Now, I'd appreciate it if you'd . . . hey! Hey!' Her voice rose as his arms closed tightly around her. 'Put me down. What are you . . .'

The man lifted her easily, curving her against his wet body, stilling her hands as she lashed out at him. Nicole's heart thudded with fear as he strode across the small cabin, towards the bunk.

'You bastard,' she yelled, 'you . . .'

But he wasn't carrying her to the bunk, he was carrying her to the ladder, shifting her over his shoulder like a sack of laundry when he reached it and carried her topside.

'OK, lady,' he snarled, dropping her on her feet, 'take a look.'

A hot wind blew Nicole's tangled hair into her face. Her hand trembled as she pushed it back and stared down at the Sunfish on its side in the water.

'I get the message,' she said, praying he couldn't hear the thud of her heart. 'You . . . you hurt my boat and you can hurt me. I . . .'

He threw up his hands. 'Are you always this dense? Look past the end of your nose for once, will you?'

She winced as his hands clamped on to her shoulders, his fingers digging into her as he twisted her unyielding body away from the sailing-boat.

'I don't see anythi . . .'

Her voice faded into silence. A barrier of rocks pierced the blue water ahead, so close they seemed almost within touching distance. Waves beat wildly against the jagged edges, sending foamy spray skywards. Nicole felt herself turn cold despite the heat of the sun and the warmth of the towelling robe. She shuddered and took an involuntary step back.

'That's right,' he said softly. He was just behind her, his head bent so that his mouth was almost at her ear. She could feel the warmth of his breath on her skin. 'Take a good look, Miss Wheeler. That's where you and your Sunfish were heading. I tried every damned thing I knew to stop you—don't you know that three blasts on a horn means danger?'

Nicole shook her head and swallowed, unable to look away from the fierce rocks and the pounding waves.

'No. I . . . I didn't realise . . . I was heading for the island, and I . . .'

'You were heading out to sea,' he said, 'with an unscheduled stop at the Dragon's Teeth first.' His fingers bit into her again as he spun her towards him. 'You didn't leave me any choice, dammit. The only way to stop you was to dump you.'

Her knees felt weak. 'I . . . I was trying to turn back. But the sheet was caught.' Her voice trembled and broke. 'It . . . it wrapped around me. Around the tiller. I couldn't turn the rudder or loosen the sail. I . . . I . . .'

'If that "macho toy" of mine hadn't been able to turn on a dime, we'd have both ended up splattered on those rocks.' A coldness filled his eyes. 'You've never sailed before, have you?'

Nicole swallowed. 'Yes. No. I mean, not alone, no. Not . . .'

He nodded. 'That's what I thought. What damned fool sold you that thing and let you take it out alone?'

'It . . . it isn't mine. It . . . it belongs to a friend . . .' She drew in her breath and looked into his eyes. 'I feel terrible,' she said softly. 'I owe you an apology.'

'Yes,' he said flatly. 'You damned well do.'

She nodded. 'I can't tell you how . . .' The words seemed to catch in her throat. She began to tremble and her eyes lifted to his. 'I . . .'

'Easy,' he said, and his voice grew soft. 'Easy, Miss Wheeler. It's all over.'

Nicole nodded. 'You're right. It's all . . .'

He caught her as she swayed forward, and his arms closed tightly around her. 'OK,' he murmured, 'just take a deep breath. That's it. And again.'

His hand cupped her head gently and brought it to his chest. The warmth of his bare skin beneath her cheek, the muscled strength of his arms and the steady beat of his heart were all an affirmation of life itself. Nicole closed her eyes and let his arms and body support her. His hand moved slowly along her back, soothing her, gentling her.

After a few minutes, she drew a deep breath. 'I'm . . . I'm all right now,' she whispered.

His hands slid to her elbows and he put her from him just enough so that he could look down into her face.

'It's over. Put it out of your mind.'

She shook her head. 'How can I? We could have . . .'

'But we didn't.'

'I can't ever tell you how sorry I am,' she whispered. 'I . . . I might have killed us both . . .'

His hands cupped her face and tilted it to his. 'Never mind that,' he said. 'We're all right. We're alive.' Nicole said nothing, and his glance fell to her mouth. 'Very much alive.' He smiled, and then he touched his mouth to hers in the lightest of kisses. 'You see?'

She looked up at him through her lashes. The sunlight played on his face, illuminating its hard planes.

'Yes,' she said softly, 'yes, I see.'

His eyes, so cold moments before, turned a warm, smoky grey. 'Do you?' he whispered, and before she could move his arms slipped around her and he bent towards her again.

Nicole's hands came up between them. 'Don't,' she said but, even as she did, her face was lifting to his. She felt the brush of his lips and then she heard a sound—a whisper, a sigh—but there was no way to know which of them had made it. Her lips parted beneath his and she tasted the sweetness of his mouth.

The world spun away. She was drowning again, but this was a different drowning, a welcome one that thickenend her blood and sent a spiral of heat through her. He gathered her against him, bringing her so close that she could feel the hard muscles of his chest pressing against her breasts and knew that his desire was as sudden and as powerful as her own. Slowly, Nicole's palms flattened against him. His heartbeat pounded beneath her hands, and the heat of his body seemed to flow into her fingertips.

A horn rent the sea-silence that surrounded them. Nicole pushed free of the man's arms and stared past him. A powerboat, small and swift, was arcing towards them, horn blasting.

'Wait,' the man whispered, but Nicole was already moving past him, staring at the boat as it drew nearer.

'Ahoy, there.'

It was Aston's voice, amplified and tense. Nicole pulled the robe around her as the boat drew abreast and cut its engines. Jimmy's face gaped at her from the stern. Aston was at the wheel. He looked from the sailing-boat lying in the water to Nicole, and then he stared at the man beside her.

'What the hell is this?' he said.

A cold smile touched the man's face. 'Powell. A pleasure, as always.'

Aston looked at Nicole again. 'Are you all right?'

'Yes,' she said quickly. Aston's face was set in a way she'd never seen before—eyes cool, mouth tight with dislike. And something more, she thought quickly, something calculating, something . . . She drew in her breath. 'I . . . I had an accident, Aston. Mr . . . Mr . . .'

The man's lips drew back in a smile. 'Tarrant,' he said softly, his eyes never leaving Aston. 'Chase Tarrant. At your service.'

Chase Tarrant. Of course! Nicole had heard the name before, falling like an oath from Aston's lips on the few occasions he lost a bid or a contract. Tarrant was a business rival, a powerful one, and Aston was sure he was dishonest.

Tarrant's glance skimmed her face. 'Don't tell me,' he said softly. 'Good old Powell is the "friend" who lent you the boat.'

Nicole flushed. 'Yes. I'm his secretary. I . . .'

'She's a hell of a lot more than that, Tarrant.'

Nicole looked at Aston in surprise. 'No,' she said, 'I . . .'

Tarrant's eyes grew even colder. 'Go on, Miss Wheeler,' he said. 'Your boyfriend's waiting for you.'

She swallowed. 'I . . . I'll send your robe to you.'

'Keep it.'

'Nicki.' Aston's voice was sharp and she turned towards him.

'Yes, all right, Aston. I'm coming. I . . . I just wanted

to thank Mr Tarrant.'

'Then do it.'

Chase Tarrant's laugh was as cold as his eyes as they slid past her and fastened on Aston.

'Oh, but she already has, Powell,' he said, and the way he said it turned Aston's face white.

Nicole shook her head. 'Aston,' she said sharply, 'don't!'

She knew she would remember the moment forever—Jimmy, wide-eyed at the stern of the motorboat; Aston, his eyes blazing with rage; Chase Tarrant, wearing the smile of a shark; and herself, frozen between them.

It was Aston who ended it. His eyes slid away from the man beside her.

'Come on, Nicki,' he said, holding out his hand. 'I'll help you.'

But, before she could take a step, Chase Tarrant swept her up into his arms. With negligent ease, he carried her to the side. His eyes glinted as he looked down at her.

'So long, sweetheart,' he said, and his mouth dropped to hers in a quick, hard kiss.

She was stunned, unable to stop him. She heard Aston's indignant voice, Jimmy's gasp, and then she was deposited gently into the motorboat.

'You . . . you . . .'

Tarrant laughed. 'Speechless, Miss Wheeler? I can hardly believe it.'

Aston put his arms around Nicole and drew her against him. She went willingly, moving into his embrace with a compliance she'd never felt before.

'Please take me home,' she said.

Tarrant's lips drew back from his teeth. 'Yes, Powell, why don't you do that? The lady's had a very strenuous morning.'

Nicole felt a tremor run through Aston's body. 'We're not finished, Tarrant,' he said softly. 'Just remember that.'

The smile faded from Tarrant's face. 'You're damned right we're not.' A terrible coldness shone in his eyes. 'You can count on it.'

Then he was gone, down the ladder and into the cabin. And, despite the sunlight and the blue sky, the empty deck of the black boat radiated a chill that made Nicole shiver.

CHAPTER TWO

NICOLE looked up from the letter she was typing and smiled at the office boy as he stepped hesitantly through the door.

'Come on in, Adam. I won't bite.'

The boy grinned. 'It's not you I'm worried about, Miss Wheeler.' He nodded towards the closed door behind her. 'Is Mr Powell in?' He moved forwards and held out a paper bag. 'I've got his lunch order here.'

Nicole nodded. 'Yes, he's in.'

The boy sighed. 'Yeah, that's what I was afraid of. I was kind of hoping he'd changed his mind and gone out.'

'Sorry,' she said lightly, 'but he's waiting for you.'

'Well, it never hurts to hope, does it?' Adam took a breath and squared his shoulders. 'OK, I'm ready. Wish me luck.'

Nicole smiled at him as she reached for the intercom. 'Don't be silly. Mr Powell's not going to bite your head off.'

'Sure he will,' the boy said with a nervous grin. 'He's been biting everybody's head off this past week. Don't tell me you've escaped, Miss Wheeler?'

Nicole's smile faded. 'I'll buzz and tell him you're here, Adam. And don't worry. Everything will be fine. You'll see.'

Minutes later, the sounds coming from behind the closed door to Aston's office proved just how wrong she'd been. Aston's voice was raised, its tone angry. When the door finally opened and Adam stepped through it, he was pale. The boy shut the door carefully behind him and shook his head.

'One more session like that one and I'm going to ask for combat pay.' He looked at Nicole with a quzzical expression. 'What's with the boss, anyway?'

Chase Tarrant, Nicole thought immediately. It was the same thing that had been wrong with Aston ever since the past weekend. But she said nothing, only smiled and held out a stack of envelopes.

'These letters have to go out as soon as possible, Adam. Would you take them to the mail-room for me, please?'

'Anything for you, Miss Wheeler.'

The boy bent towards her as he took the letters from her outstretched hand. 'Good luck with the boss,' he whispered. 'You're going to need it.'

The sound of the intercom buzzer interrupted him. Nicole pressed the button and Aston's voice, sharp and demanding, pierced the room.

'Nicole? Get in here, will you?'

Nicole managed a smile as she rose from her chair. 'I'll see you later, Adam.'

She waited until the boy was gone, and then she strode purposefully to Aston's closed door, knocked once, then opened it. Aston's leather chair was turned away from her; he sat staring out of the wide expanse of window-wall behind his desk. At the sound of the door closing, he swivelled towards her.

'There you are,' he said. The edge in his voice made her spine stiffen. 'Doesn't that kid ever get anything right? I've told him a dozen times not to order my lunch from the café on the corner. They have the lousiest coffee. And another thing. They . . .'

'*I* phoned it in, Aston,' she said quietly. 'You decided to lunch in at the last minute, and that's the only place that would deliver in less than an hour.'

Aston looked at her. 'Well,' he said finally, 'I just hope they got the orders straight. They never do.'

There was a petulance in his voice that scraped against Nicole's nerve-endings like a fingernail against a blackboard, but she forced a smile to her lips.

'Let's take a look, shall we?' The bag parted beneath her fingers and she began taking small parcels from its depths. 'One chicken sandwich,' she said, unwrapping it and setting it on his desk. 'One ham sandwich with mustard. Pickles. A sweet roll. Two coffees.' She frowned and peered into the bag. 'Actually, they do seem to have forgotten something.'

Aston's eyebrows drew together. 'What did I tell you? I knew they would. What is it?'

Nicole's eyes met his. 'Hemlock. It's what half the staff wishes you'd drink, Aston. You've given everyone a dreadful few days.'

She'd hoped her lightly teasing words would make him smile. But they didn't; they only seemed to make him angrier. His scowl deepened.

'Who's been complaining?' he demanded. 'Give me their names and I'll . . .'

'You'll what? Yell? You've done enough of that to last a lifetime. Fire them? You're lucky half the people who work here haven't quit. You have a loyal staff here, Aston, but you're going to drive them away. They all say the same thing, and you can't blame them for . . .'

'I don't think it's too much to expect a little loyalty from you, Nicki,' he said stiffly. 'I should think you wouldn't permit people to say unpleasant things about me in front of you.'

'They've said nothing but the truth,' Nicole said bluntly. 'You've been unpleasant to everybody all week. And you can't fault them for speaking openly to me. They know I work directly for you, and everybody's trying to make sense of your behaviour.'

His eyes met hers. 'That's not what I meant.'

'I haven't flaunted our relationship, Aston. You know that. I doubt if anyone even knows you and I see each other away from the office.'

Aston smiled unpleasantly. 'Relationship? I'd hardly call it that.'

Nicole's eyes narrowed until the hazel irises glinted with gold. 'Aston,' she said softly, 'don't do this. You've pushed me and pushed me this past week, and all you've done is convince me that I was right all along. I said months ago that I didn't think we should see each other outside the office. Do you remember? I told you I . . .'

Two spots of colour appeared high on his cheeks, a stark contrast to his pale skin and pale hair.

'Oh, yes, Nicki, I remember it quite clearly. You were the very soul of propriety. You said you didn't believe in mixing business and pleasure. It took me months to change your mind and get you to agree to dinner. And then it was another two weeks before you'd call me by my first name and two weeks more before you'd let me kiss you goodnight.'

Nicole put down her coffee-container. 'Is this the reason you sent for me, Aston? Because if it is . . .'

'But you weren't so proper when it came to Chase Tarrant, were you? You . . . Nicki? Nicki!' His voice rose as she strode rapidly across the office. 'Where do you think you're going?'

'I'm going to have my lunch in peace. We've been over and over this . . .'

Aston crossed the room quickly and grasped her arm. 'And I haven't got a satisfactory answer out of you yet. What was going on between you and that s.o.b.?'

Nicole's eyes went from his hand on her arm to his face. 'Let go of me,' she said softly.

His hand curled more tightly around her for a second and then it dropped to his side.

'I asked you a simple question,' he said.

'And I've answered it a dozen times. Nothing was going on. The man saved my life. He . . .'

'He dumped you into the water, Nicki. That story about saving you . . .'

She sighed. 'It wasn't a story, Aston. You saw the rocks as well as I did. I'd have gone right into them.'

Aston ran his hand through his hair. 'All right, all right. But that doesn't explain the rest. You knew Chase Tarrant five minutes before you were in his arms, kissing him as if . . . as if . . .'

Nicole felt her cheeks flush with colour. 'I don't have to explain anything to you. But I have, all week long. I told you, what you saw was—it was just Tarrant's idea of a bad joke. It had nothing to do with me.'

'Come on, Nicole, I wasn't born yesterday! You were kissing him while Jimmy and I were coming towards his boat. We could see you, for goodness' sake. And then it happened again, just before he handed you over to me.'

'Handed me over to you?' Nicole's voice was dangerously soft. 'Like a package, you mean?'

Powell flushed. 'You know what I mean, Nicki. You and Tarrant . . .'

Nicole drew a deep breath. 'Listen to me, Aston. This is the last time I'm going to say this. The man saved my life. That's the only positive thing I can say about him. Other than that, he's an . . . an egomaniac, and I refuse to be held accountable for his actions. You told me yourself he's not to be trusted.'

The spots of colour faded from Aston's cheeks. The strange expression that twisted across his face was the same as it had been the day he'd found her on Chase Tarrant's boat. As quickly as it appeared, it vanished, and he nodded.

'That's right, he isn't. He's a scoundrel. He's won bids from under my nose by paying off the right people; he's cut costs by using shoddy materials.'

'I just don't understand how he gets away with it. Why doesn't somebody blow the whistle on him?'

Powell's eyes slid away from hers. 'He's a shrewd operator, Nicki. Most of what he does is hard to prove. But that's how he built that company of his. Everybody knows it, just as they know that under all that expensive patina, the club memberships and the fast boats, he's still just a ditch-digger with dirt under his finger-nails . . .'

'At least it was honest dirt, Powell.'

The deep male voice startled them both. They swung towards the door and Nicole's breath caught. Chase Tarrant stood in the open doorway, one shoulder leaning casually against the jamb, a cool smile on his face. Dressed in a charcoal flannel suit, he was just as broad-shouldered and imposing as he'd been the last time she'd seen him.

He smiled lazily, knotted his hand into a loose fist, and examined his neatly trimmed, buffed nails.

'No, no dirt there. I haven't dug a ditch in more than ten years,' he said. 'Not with a shovel, anyway. I admit I do get out there and operate one of my 'dozers now and then. I like to keep my hand in. You ought to try it, Powell.' His eyes locked on Aston's stunned face. 'You might pick up a smudge or two but, hell, you won't mind that. Your hands are dirtier than mine ever were.'

'Who let you in here?' Aston demanded. 'How did you . . .?'

Tarrant shrugged. 'Your secretary wasn't at her desk.' He glanced at Nicole, and another smile curved lazily at his mouth. 'Although I don't imagine you spend much time out there, Miss Wheeler. This is a much more cosy arrangement.'

A crimson flush spread over Nicole's cheeks, and she turned away from his leering smile.

'I'll call for security, Aston,' she said, reaching for the phone.

Powell nodded. 'Go on, Nicki. Phone down and tell them we want this man thrown out.'

Tarrant laughed softly. 'Yeah,' he said, his eyes never leaving Aston, 'go on, Nicki.' Nicole's flush deepened; somehow, the way he used her nickname turned it into an insult. 'Make the call, by all means. But phone everybody, not just security. The yacht club officials, the reporters covering the Coral City to Barbados Race . . . Call them all. Tell them old Aston and I are going to have a little chat about *Enchantress* and we'd love some company.' His eyes grew cold. 'Wouldn't we, Powell?'

Aston's hand closed over Nicole's. 'Wait,' he whispered.

Nicole stared at him. 'Wait? But . . .'

'What do you know about *Enchantress,* Tarrant?'

Chase smiled lazily. 'Aren't you going to ask me to sit down?' When there was no answer, he shrugged and walked into the room.

Nicole watched him as he strolled casually around the large, well-appointed office. He wasn't really taller than Aston, she thought crazily. Then why did he seem to fill the room?

'Nice,' he said, looking at a Wyeth painting hanging on the panelled wall. He walked to the massive rosewood and teak desk, touched it lightly then ran his hand over the back of one of the pair of Eames chairs drawn up opposite the desk. 'Very nice. It's wonderful what all that old money will buy, isn't it?' His voice roughened. 'Isn't it, Powell?'

'What do you want here, Tarrant? I'm not going to play games with you . . .'

Chase grinned wolfishly. 'But you're good at games, old man.' His eyes went to Nicole and then back to Aston. 'Did you ever tell her how you won the Bretton Trophy a couple of years ago?'

Nicole watched that strange expression flicker over Aston's face again. 'I asked what you wanted,' he said softly.

'I bet you never told her how you won the regatta last year, either. Did he tell you that, Miss Wheeler?' Nicole said nothing and he smiled, but it was a smile that never reached his eyes. 'I guess modesty kept you silent, hmm?'

Aston's face was white. 'Get out,' he whispered.

'Are you as modest about your business successes, Powell? I'll bet you are. I'll bet she doesn't know how you managed that magical underbid for the Park Plaza mall or the Macombs Road office complex or . . .'

Aston's voice was like a whip. 'Wait outside, Nicki.'

'What's he talking about?' she said. 'Aston?'

'I said to wait outside.'

Chase moved quickly towards her and curled his hand around her wrist, his cool fingers gripping her like steel.

'Stay where you are, Miss Wheeler,' he said softly. 'I might need a witness to what comes next.'

Nicole stared blankly at him. His words were frightening, but not as much as the aggressive thrust of his jaw or the coiled tension she felt emanating from his hand.

She turned helplessly towards Aston. 'Shall I call security?'

But he didn't answer. His eyes, dark smudges against the pasty whiteness of his skin, were fixed on Chase. He ran his tongue across his lips before he spoke.

'What is it you want?'

Chase grinned. 'Only what's rightfully mine, old man.' The deceptive lightness of his words were a frightening contrast to the steel grey flash of his eyes. 'I want *Enchantress*.'

Aston laughed. 'You're crazy.'

'Turn her over to me, Powell, and no one will be the wiser. Otherwise . . .'

'You *are* crazy! Turn her over to you? I've spent a fortune on that boat. It's taken me eight months to have her built . . .'

Chase dropped Nicole's hand and took a step forward. 'You're breaking my heart, Powell,' he said in a softly ominous voice. 'It took me two years to have her designed, and heaven only knows how many years before that, hoping and planning and sweating until I could afford . . .'

'Look, Tarrant, I don't know what kind of scam you're trying to pull, but you can save your breath. *I* funded the design. *I* sweated out the trials, *I* built the boat that's going to win the Coral City to Barbados Race. Now get the hell out of here before I . . .'

'That's very good. If I didn't know the truth, I'd be tempted to believe you. But you forgot something, Powell. The man who can be bought once can be bought twice.' Chase's voice was soft as smoke. 'Your man came to me; he figured he could double his money by telling me his story.' He smiled. 'He gave me a sworn statement, Powell. I know everything.'

Nicole drew in her breath. 'What's he talking about, Aston? Is it the Mystery Boat? The one you commissioned for the race?'

'Don't listen to him, Nicki. The man's a liar. He . . .'

'When I found out you'd had the plans for my boat stolen, that you were building her duplicate, I wanted to beat your head in.' He laughed softly. 'But that was nothing new—hell, I've wanted to do that for years, each time you cheated me.' A cold smile came and went across his face. 'And then I thought of a much better plan, Powell. I decided I'd let your lying and your cheating work to my advantage for once. I decided I'd let you build my boat for me.'

Nicole's eyes widened in astonishment. The man was incredible! He was arrogant, lying, bullying—it was a miracle Aston hadn't had him thrown out five minutes ago. No wonder he despised Chase Tarrant!

'Why are you even bothering to listen to this nonsense?' she demanded angrily. 'Call security. Better still, call the police. Have him arrested for trespass. And libel, and . . . and . . .'

Chase laughed. 'That's one hell of a good idea, Powell. Why don't we do that? Call the cops and . . .'

'No.' Aston's voice was sharp. Nicole looked at him in surprise, and he gave her a quick smile. 'No,' he said again, this time more softly. 'That's just what he wants, Nicki. Don't you see?' His eyes narrowed darkly. 'If we call the police in, the papers will get hold of the story. He knows I can't afford any publicity right now, not with the Taft Centre on the drawing-board.'

Nicole shook her head. 'But surely . . .'

'Tarrant lost the bid for that contract to me. That's what this is all about, Nicki. He knows exactly what he's doing. It's a municipal contract, and this is an election year. The mayor and the city council will find a way to worm out of a deal that draws negative publicity.'

Chase nodded. 'That's good, Powell,' he said softly. 'Very creative.'

Aston looked at Nicole. 'He can't lose, Nicki. Either he gets my boat or he gets the Taft Centre by default. Don't you see?'

She shook her head again. 'No, I *don't* see. You can't just hand your boat over to him. Why, that's—that's theft. No one would believe that trumped-up story of his! He simply paid somebody to perjure himself.'

'You're right, of course,' Aston said quickly. 'But I can't run the risk. The race is only two days away, and it's drawn a lot of publicity. A story like this would make a juicy headline. The papers would play it up.'

'Yes,' Nicole said impatiently, 'but you can prove the boat's yours. You can . . .'

'I can take him to court and go through an endless round of subpoenas and questions and answers and, in the end, I'd win. Of course I would. But it would be too late by then. The mayor and the city councilmen would be reeling, the company would have suffered a black eye . . .'

'Yes, but so would he. He's got as much to lose as you do.'

Aston shook his head. 'I'm the one with the municipal contract, Nicki. I'm the one with the old name, the reputation . . .'

Chase slapped his hand on the desk. 'Enough!' he growled. 'Spin this fairy-tale on your own time, Powell, not mine. I've got a lot to do in the next couple of days. Have your lawyer send the transfer papers to my office.' He reached into his pocket, pulled out a piece of paper, and tossed it on the desk. 'That's a cheque for the cost of building *Enchantress*—less the cost of her design.' His lips drew back from his teeth. 'I wouldn't want you to go around saying bad things about me.'

Nicole stared at Aston. 'Tell him to take it back,' she said slowly. 'Aston, please . . .'

A muscle twitched in Aston's cheek. He snatched the cheque and stuffed it into his pocket.

'I promise you, Tarrant, I'll get even with you if it's

the last thing I do.'

Nicole shrank back as Chase moved past her like a cat going for the kill. In one swift motion, he grasped Aston by the shirtfront and dragged him forwards until their faces were only inches apart.

'You don't know how right you are, Powell,' he said. His voice was low, thick with something so fearsome it made Nicole's blood run cold. 'If you try anything, it sure as hell *will* be the last thing you do.' His fingers tightened on the shirt; above the twisted silk, Aston's face was a pale oval. 'Do you understand me? It's payback time.'

Aston's eyes shone with fear. Nicole didn't blame him for it—Chase Tarrant was like a man possessed. Yet, in some dark corner of her mind, a little voice was whispering, asking her why Aston allowed himself to be intimidated. No one would ever get away with intimidating Chase Tarrant.

The thought was so disloyal that she hated herself for it. Quickly, she pushed her way between the two men.

'Get out of here,' she said. Her eyes fastened on Chase's. 'Get out, or I'll call security whether Aston wants me to or not.'

Chase's smile was cool. He let go of the other man's shirt, lifting his hands away with deliberate care

'I'm almost finished here, anyway,' he said, and then he looked at Nicole. Her pulse began to race. There was something in his eyes, a message meant for her alone.

'No,' she whispered, shrinking back. But it was too late. He reached out and ran his hand lightly along her jaw. 'I hate you,' she said. 'I only wish . . . I wish . . .'

He smiled; for a moment, they were alone again on his boat, with the heat of the sun beating down on them.

'What do you wish?' he asked softly.

She wanted to tell him she wished she'd never laid

eyes on him, but his hand was moving along her cheek, slipping into her hair, his fingers tangling in the tumble of curls. She heard Aston's voice, heard the anger in it, but whatever he was saying seemed to come from a great distance. Her eyes were riveted to Chase's, to their winter-morning grey. When he drew her to him she whimpered softly, and then his mouth touched hers, brushing it with flame.

Time and reality slipped away. The kiss might have lasted for an instant or for all of eternity. Nicole knew only that she was breathless when finally he let her go.

There was silence in the office, and then Aston made a strangled sound deep in his throat.

'I'll kill you for this, Tarrant,' he said.

The sound of his voice set her free. She turned and put her hand on his arm. 'No,' she said, 'don't, Aston. He isn't worth it.'

Chase Tarrant's lips twisted in a tight smile. 'Listen to the lady, Powell. She makes sense.'

He slammed the door behind him, and silence filled the office again.

CHAPTER THREE

'WOULD you care to see our dessert menu, sir?'

Aston looked at Nicole, who smiled and shook her head. 'None for me, thanks. But I would like some more coffee.'

'The same for me,' Aston said.

They sat silently while the waiter refilled their cups. As soon as he moved off, Nicole leaned across the table.

'Are you certain you want to go to the reception at the yacht club, Aston? Won't there be a million questions?'

'About Tarrant sailing my boat tomorrow?' Aston shrugged. 'No, not really. I told you, I've already spread the word about my "injury".' He glanced down at his left arm, caught up in a black silk sling that matched the lapels of his dinner-jacket. 'Everybody was most sympathetic when they heard I'd dislocated my shoulder playing racquetball.'

Nicole sighed. 'I just can't believe Chase Tarrant agreed to go along with that story.'

'Why wouldn't he? All he cares about is winning.' A cold smile came and went on his face. 'And he thinks he has.'

'And what about everybody else, Aston? Will they believe you'd give that man your boat?'

He drew a cigarette case from his breast pocket. Light danced across its Florentined gold surface.

'Why not, given the circumstances?' He put a cigarette in his mouth and thumbed a flame from a gold and silver lighter. 'Everyone knows how badly I wanted to see

Enchantress in this race. And I suspect the fact that Tarrant gave me a cheque to cover her cost has made the rounds by now.'

'But no one knows that.'

Aston smiled. 'Bankers aren't quite as discreet as they pretend, Nicki. I deposited the cheque in my account yesterday, which means there have been two full days for the story to spread.' Two thin streams of smoke drifted from his nostrils. 'Tarrant's not a fool; he wanted the deal to all look very above-board and proper, and it does.'

Nicole's hazel eyes darkened. 'The way it looks doesn't change the truth, Aston. He stole your boat. He blackmailed you, he threatened you . . .'

Aston nodded. 'I haven't forgotten,' he said softly. 'Believe me, I've thought of little else since it happened.'

Nicole drew a deep breath. 'Oh,' she whispered, 'how I hate him!'

'Do you, Nicki?'

She looked up, wondering at the seeming sharpness in Aston's voice. But the expression on his face was open and pleasant, and she nodded.

'Yes, of course.'

Aston reached across the table and covered her hand with his. 'Don't worry about a thing, my dear. I promise you, I'll take care of Mr Tarrant.'

'Yes, I know what you said. After the race, when all the hoo-ha's died down. But I still don't think that's going to work, Aston. The more time that passes, the harder it will be to prove anything. And what if he wins? Have you considered that?'

'He won't.'

Nicole shook her head. 'Just suppose he does,' she said stubbornly. 'Can you imagine how it will look if you try to press charges against the winner?'

'Tarrant's never won against me yet,' Aston said

sharply. 'He won't win this time, either.'

'You can't be positive of that. You told me how much money you put into the boat's design. If it's really that innovative . . .'

His fingers tightened on hers. 'I'm telling you, Tarrant will lose.'

'I hope you're right, Aston. I just wish you'd . . .'

'Nicki,' his hand tightened on hers and she looked up at him, 'let's talk about something more pleasant, shall we?' Aston smiled. 'You look lovely tonight, my dear.'

She smiled. 'Thank you.'

Aston let go of her hand. 'That green's a perfect colour for you,' he said, reaching into his pocket. 'I hope this complements it well.'

She frowned as he put a long velvet box on the table between them. 'Is that for me?'

Aston laughed. 'It's certainly not for the waiter, Nicki. Well, aren't you going to open it?'

'Aston, I hope you haven't . . .'

'Go on,' he said, 'open it. Please.'

Nicole picked up the box and lifted the lid. Green and white fire seemed to leap into the light.

'What . . .' She looked from the emerald and diamond necklace to the man opposite her. 'Aston, for goodness' sake, what is this?'

'Do you like it?' He laughed at the bewildered expression on her face. 'The colour's right, after all. It's a perfect match to your dress.'

'Aston.' Nicole cleared her throat. 'Aston, when you asked me what colour dress I was going to wear, I thought you meant you were going to send me flowers. But this . . .' Her eyes sought his. 'You know I can't accept this,' she said. 'I've told you and told you . . .'

'I want to buy you pretty things, Nicki. It's my pleasure.'

'But it's not my pleasure to accept them, Aston.' Nicole heard the edge to her voice and she forced herself to take a deep breath. 'Thank you, but you'll have to take it back.'

There was a silence. Aston was angry; Nicole knew him well enough to sense it, even if nothing showed on his face. Why didn't he stop doing this? she wondered. It was a pattern that had begun after she'd turned down his first marriage proposal. He would offer some extravagant gift, she would turn it down, he'd be irritated, and then it would all pass over. Until the next time. And there always was a next time.

But tonight was different. Instead of glowering, he sighed. 'All right,' he said, stabbing out his cigarette, 'I'll take it back.'

Nicole looked at him in surprise. 'Well,' she said with a little laugh, 'thank you. I'm glad you're not . . .'

'I do have one favour to ask, Nicki.' He smiled again and lifted the necklace from its box. 'Wear it tonight.'

She shook her head. 'I couldn't do that.'

'Please, Nicki. You'd be doing me a favour. I can't walk around with that box in my pocket all night. It's going to be crowded as hell at the club, and, well, you know how I am sometimes. The thought of losing this is upsetting. The safest place for it is on your neck.'

'Aston, I can't. You shouldn't have . . .'

'You're right, I shouldn't have.' He smiled winningly. 'But I did. I promise, I've learned my lesson, Nicki. Just do this for me tonight and I won't do anything like it again.' He laughed softly. 'Come on, how can you pass up an offer like that? "I, Aston Powell, do swear and affirm that I shall never, ever again try and bedazzle Nicole Wheeler with gifts of fabulous jewels, expensive furs, or other luxuries. I promise to buy her only boxes of chocolates . . ." '

Nicole laughed. 'Plain, not milk.' When he nodded, she

sighed. 'All right, I'll babysit your necklace. But I'll be a nervous wreck until I take it off.'

For a moment, Aston's eyes seemed to glitter with the same cold fire as the jewels in his hand.

'Thank you, Nicki. You can't imagine how happy you've made me.'

She took the necklace from him and fastened it around her throat. The gold setting felt cold against her skin, the stones unnaturally heavy.

'I was edgy enough about tonight as it was.' Her hand went to the necklace. 'And now there's this . . .'

'Are you concerned about seeing Chase Tarrant again?'

Nicole nodded. 'How can you bear the thought of being in the same room with him,' she said softly, 'of pretending you've willingly entered into a deal with him . . .?'

'It will all work out in the end, Nicki. I promise.'

'I suppose you're right. It's just that—well, I don't understand how he can get away with the things he does. Now that you've told me all about him . . .'

'The man's clever. He knows how to manipulate situations and people to his own advantage, and he always covers his tracks well. But he won't get away with what he's done to me.' A muscle knotted in his jaw. 'I still see him touching you when I close my eyes.'

Nicole looked down at the table. 'I don't want to talk about it,' she said quickly.

'Handling you, in front of me!'

'Aston, please . . .'

'I don't know why I didn't understand from the beginning. Tarrant only kissed you because it was a slap in my face.'

The muscles in her face felt stiff. 'Yes, I know.'

'He was telling me I couldn't hold on to my own woman.'

Nicole drew in her breath. 'Aston,' she said sharply, 'I

don't want to discuss this. I . . .'

He lit another cigarette and drew the smoke deep into his lungs. 'I've never hated anyone the way I hate Chase Tarrant,' he said softly. 'When I think of what he's done to me . . .'

Nicole pushed back her chair. 'If we're going to the reception, we'd better get started. It's getting late, isn't it?'

Aston nodded and signalled to their waiter. 'By the minute,' he said, and he began to chuckle. He was still laughing as he settled their bill.

Nicole watched in silence, wishing she could find something to laugh about. It had been difficult to smile the past couple of days. She couldn't seem to stop thinking about Chase Tarrant, and how completely and thoroughly he'd humiliated her.

She stood as Aston held out her raincoat. His hands brushed her shoulders as he settled it on her, and she thought of Tarrant's hands as they'd closed on her that day in Aston's office. Would she ever be able to put the memory aside?

She knew Aston was right about why Tarrant had kissed her; she'd known it all along. Those kisses had been barbed messages from one male to another. Tarrant thought she was Aston's property, and that made her fair game.

Aston touched her arm as they stepped into the cool, rainy night. 'Wait here until I get the car, Nicki.'

She nodded and turned up the collar of her raincoat. Aston was so blind. He kept talking about his humiliation at having to watch while Chase Tarrant kissed her. If he only knew the truth—that she hadn't just suffered Tarrant's caresses but had melted beneath them, that her mouth had blossomed beneath his and her body had risen to his touch.

The worst of it was that Tarrant knew. She had seen the

flash of awareness in his eyes, felt it in the hardening of his body as it pressed against hers. It was as if she and he shared a terrible secret, one that burned within her breast like a cold flame.

She'd told herself there were reasons to explain her response. The first time he'd kissed her, she'd been in shock from her near-drowning. The next, she'd been frightened by the violent scene in Aston's office. She couldn't be held responsible for her behaviour under those conditions.

But it was still impossible to look at herself in the mirror without flinching, just as understanding why Tarrant had used her didn't make her hate him any less. And she did understand. She'd had three years' experience with a man like him, one who had to win at any cost, no matter who was hurt in the process.

Winning was everything to such men. The only way to deal with them was to beat them at their own game. Tony had never given her the chance, and neither would Chase Tarrant. His game was with Aston—she was a pawn, not a player—and Aston, damn him, would refuse to believe how serious the game was until it was too late to matter.

'Nicki?' Aston's black Mercedes was pulled to the kerb. He smiled as she hurried into it. 'You looked as if you were a million miles away,' he said as he pulled out into the road.

'I . . . I was thinking about the race tomorrow. Will they hold it if this rain keeps up?'

He laughed. 'The only thing that would stop the race would be nuclear war, and I'm not even sure about that.' He grimaced as he turned up the speed of the windscreen wipers. 'For all I care it can rain cats and dogs. I'll be sitting in the clubhouse, having coffee.'

Nicole ran her fingers through her damp hair and fluffed it away from her face. 'I didn't realise you were planning on being there, Aston.'

He shrugged. 'It won't look right unless I'm on hand to wish Tarrant *bon voyage.*'

'It won't look right anyway,' she said, and she held up her hand before he could answer. 'I know, I know. You think people will buy your story. But people must know how much you two dislike each other.'

'Even nations have been known to put aside disagreements in the name of sport, Nicki.'

'I suppose.' She sat silently as the car sped through the dark, rain-slicked streets, and then she turned towards Aston again. 'I just wish . . .'

'Will you stop worrying your pretty head over this?' He smiled at her as he braked at a red light. 'I'll take care of everything,' he said, patting her knee. 'But it's nice to know you care about my welfare, Nicki.'

She smiled back at him. 'Of course I care.'

His palm slid slowly up her leg, under her skirt towards her thigh. 'I have a wonderful idea. Why don't we announce our engagement tonight, hmm? That would take the spotlight off the race for a while.'

Nicole's hand closed firmly over his and stilled it. 'No,' she said quickly. 'I . . . I mean, I'm not ready for that, Aston. I told you, I need time. I'm not sure I . . .'

She looked down at his hand, still resting on her flesh. It felt warm and somehow alien, and she thought suddenly of the first summer she'd lived in Coral City and she'd awakened during the night to find a large palmetto bug crawling on her skin.

A shudder ran through her. She pulled his hand away from her leg and put it on the steering wheel.

'You'll need it to drive,' she said with forced lightness. 'You're supposed to be disabled, remember?'

Aston said nothing. She heard the sound of his breathing, and then the light changed to green and he stepped down hard on the accelerator.

'I'll be glad when this damned race is over,' he muttered, and the car shot ahead into the darkness.

The reception was in full swing by the time they arrived. At first, Nicole kept scanning the room for Chase Tarrant while a cold knot tightened beneath her breast. The thought of having to see the man again, of having to pretend to be cordial to him, was enough to make her ill.

After a while, the fear began to ease. Everyone who could wangle an invitation to the party seemed to have done so. Only Chase was missing.

'What did I tell you, Nicki?' Aston smiled as he sipped some champagne. 'The man knows he's out of his depth here.'

'But he's a member, isn't he?'

Aston laughed. 'A member, yes, but a newcomer.'

'I thought you said he'd lived here for ten years.'

'Precisely.' He patted her shoulder. 'He's probably busy trying to put *Enchantress* in order at the last minute. Not that it will help him.'

They made slow progress across the crowded room. People stood packed into little groups. There was lots of talk about the Caribbean and the Mediterranean ports. You had to shout to make yourself heard, and after a few minutes Nicole gave up trying. She had little to say, anyway. She'd never spent a winter on the Costa del Sol or cruised the waters off Tahiti, and no one seemed interested in talking about much else.

Every now and then someone stared at her throat. It was disconcerting until she remembered the emerald and diamond necklace, and then she'd put her hand to it, reassuring herself it was still there. Even in a room filled with bejewelled women, Aston's would-be gift stood out. Nicole found herself wishing there were a way to announce that it wasn't hers.

Aston kept his arm around her as they moved from group to group. His hand lay heavy on her waist, the fingers splayed along her hip in a gesture that somehow annoyed her. It seemed, she thought, almost proprietorial, and then she told herself that she was being foolish. He was just trying to keep her from being bumped and shoved by the crowd.

He told everyone about his unfortunate racquetball injury, adding to the story as the evening wore on, until he was describing in detail a shoulder-slam into the wall and the excruciating pain that followed. Nicole was surprised to find herself at first embarrassed and then irritated at the story. But Aston's listeners were invariably sympathetic.

'What a pity, Powell,' people kept saying. 'Damned shame.'

Aston nodded and sighed and said yes, it was too bad, wasn't it, but wasn't it good luck for him that the Tarrant boat had run into difficulties. And, as he'd predicted, everyone accepted the story. Only one man expressed surprise that he and Chase Tarrant had struck a deal.

'Well, we buried the hatchet,' Aston said blandly.

The man laughed. 'I'm just amazed you didn't bury it in each other.'

Aston laughed heartily. 'Now, George, you know how it is. I've put a hell of a lot of time and money into *Enchantress*. I wanted to recoup something, after all. It's just too bad someone as—well, you know, someone like Tarrant had to profit by my bad luck.'

And then he deftly changed the subject to a discussion of the chances of a French-built sloop finishing in the top three places.

'I saw her race off the Cap d'Antibes last winter,' someone said, and soon the group was discussing the latest gossip about the French Riviera. After a while, Nicole's lips hurt from the effort not to yawn. She patted Aston's arm and slipped it free of her waist.

'I'll be right back,' she whispered, and before he could say anything she slid into a hole in the crowd.

She fought her way across the floor, trying not to step on too many toes. There was an area far from the bar and the buffet that seemed a bit less crowded; if she could just get there and spend a little time not listening to talk of Bebe and Didi and the Cap d'Antibes . . .

An arm slid around her waist. 'Coming through,' a deep voice said.

The man drew her closer, moulding her body to his, and she knew at once it was Chase Tarrant. Her pulse began to race.

'Let go of me,' she said quickly.

'Don't be foolish, Miss Wheeler. I'm just being helpful.'

'Let go,' she repeated, 'or I'll . . .'

'People are watching,' he said mildly. 'How will it look if you and I start a tug of war? You don't want to blow your boyfriend's story, do you?'

'No one's watching us,' Nicole hissed, but it wasn't true. Women were; she saw their admiring glances drift over the man beside her, darkly handsome in dinner-jacket and ruffled shirt, then move dismissively to her.

'Try smiling at me,' he said, and when she did, he laughed. 'I've seen sweeter smiles on jack o'lanterns at Hallowe'en. But if that's the best you can manage, it'll have to do.' His arm tightened around her. 'We want everyone to think the three of us are the best of pals, don't we, Nicole?'

When they reached an open space on the far side of the room, she pulled free of his arm and snatched a glass of champagne from a passing waiter.

'Your arrangements with Aston are none of my business,' she said coolly.

Chase reached for one of the fluted glasses and smiled at her. 'Where is Powell tonight?' His eyes moved over her with slow insolence. 'He has the damnedest habit of letting you stray.'

She felt a rush of heat to her face. 'Mr Tarrant . . .'

'Chase.' He smiled again. 'Surely we're on a first-name basis by now?'

'Mr Tarrant,' she said carefully, 'I really don't have very much to say to you. If you'll excuse me . . .'

'Of course, Miss Wheeler. I'm sure you're in a hurry to get back to the others. Which scandal are they on now? The one about Didi losing her bikini bottom at the Cap d'Antibes?'

Nicole looked at him in surprise, and he laughed. 'I've heard all the stories. Only the names and places ever change. Dull as hell, isn't it?'

She knew it was; it was what had driven her away from Aston and his friends, but thinking it seemed disloyal now. Nicole shrugged.

'I have no idea,' she said carefully. 'I was thinking of Aston. He's probably looking for me.'

'I doubt it. He's too busy winning the Purple Heart and the Victoria Cross for his dislocated shoulder.'

A little wave of guilt went through her. 'He's just trying to make it sound realistic, Mr Tarrant. I should think you'd be grateful he decided to let you get away with blackmail.'

Chase's eyebrows rose. 'Is that what you really think he's doing?'

'I think he's a fool to let you get away with anything,' she said coldly. 'And now, if you'll excuse me . . .'

He caught her hand. 'Aren't you going to wish me luck for tomorrow?'

Nicole looked at him. 'I hope your boat sinks under

you, Mr Tarrant,' she said clearly. 'I hope it never even leaves its mooring.'

Chase grinned. 'Ah, Nicole, Nicole, does your boy-friend know what a treasure you are?'

'Mr Tarrant . . .'

'He's not the kind of man you need.'

He was laughing at her, damn him! 'My relationship with Aston Powell is none of your business, Mr Tarrant. I . . .'

His fingers flicked lightly against the emerald and diamond necklace. 'A little token of Powell's admiration, Nicole?'

She didn't even hesitate. 'Yes,' she said defiantly.

His eyes darkened to smoke. 'Come with me.'

Nicole looked at him blankly. 'What?'

He caught her hand in his. She felt the press of his fingers against the soft underside of her wrist. When he spoke, his voice was a whisper.

'My car is just outside.'

Nicole swallowed. 'What are you talking about? Aston . . .'

'To hell with Aston.'

She felt the leap of her pulse. 'I don't . . . I don't understand.'

His eyes were hot on hers. 'I want to make love to you. It's what you want, too.'

She shook her head. He was crazy. Of course he was. This was Chase Tarrant. Her enemy. Aston's enemy. Aston . . .

Her hand went to her throat, to Aston's necklace. The coldness of the stones pressed against her overheated flesh.

'Get away from me,' she said in a shaky voice.

Chase laughed softly. 'You don't mean that.'

Nicole nodded. 'I do,' she said quickly. 'I . . . I'm here with Aston.'

'Are you in love with him?'

'Yes.'

'You're lying, Nicole.'

Chase's arms closed around her. 'No,' she said, 'damn you! Don't . . .'

The room spun away as his mouth took hers. Her hands came up between them, but when she felt his arms tighten around her, when she felt the hard press of his powerful body against hers, she was lost. As if she were bewitched, she lifted her arms and wound them tightly around his neck, raising herself on tiptoe until her breasts were flattened against his chest, until she felt the strong beat of his heart drumming against hers. She moaned softly as his hand moved along her back, stroking her, caressing her so that she felt the heat of his fingers through her dress.

'Nicole!'

Aston's voice was as sharp as a shard of broken glass. Nicole's eyes opened wide. She slammed her hands against Chase's chest, shoving against him with all her strength. The sounds of the crowd, sounds that had vanished when he kissed her, wrapped around her with deadly speed—the muted laughter, the delighted whispers, the rustle of fabric as people jostled for a clearer look at the spectacle unfolding before them.

Slowly, she turned towards Aston. He was standing beside her, white-lipped with rage, his eyes fixed on her face.

'Aston,' she whispered. 'I . . . I'm so sorry. I don't know how . . .'

'It's not really her fault, Powell.' Chase's voice was cool. 'Don't blame her.'

'Tarrant,' Aston whispered. 'Tarrant, I'll kill you for this. I'll . . .'

Nicole flinched as Chase reached towards her, but it was only to run his hand along the emeralds and diamonds that lay cold against her flesh. 'Women and boats are alike,' he said softly. 'Anybody can buy them, but it takes a man to make them perform.'

The crowd gasped. Nicole felt the blood drain from her face. She looked at Aston, waiting, waiting—but he stood silent. At last, she took a step towards the man who had humiliated her beyond endurance. When she spoke, her voice was so low it was a whisper.

'You'll pay for this,' she said. 'You'll pay, I swear it.'

Chase made her a mocking bow. 'Thank you for the offer, Miss Wheeler. But your value is diminished by the company you keep.'

The crowd parted as he walked towards it, then closed after him. Silence hung in the room; then there was an explosion of voices. Nicole looked from one amused face to another, and then she spun away and forced a path through the room, not pausing until she reached the exit door.

'Nicki!'

Aston's voice rasped behind her. She slammed through the door, shivering in the sudden coolness of the night and the rain.

'Nicki, wait.' Aston grasped her arm and turned her towards him. 'There was nothing I could do,' he said. 'But he won't win. I promise.'

Nicole pulled away from his hand. 'No,' she said in a clear, cold voice, 'he damned well won't.'

CHAPTER FOUR

ENCHANTRESS swung at her mooring, her sleek hull responding to the touch of current and wind. Rain pelted her teakwood deck and furled sails, as it had throughout the night. In the east, dawn brushed the sky, a yellowish bruise against the grey of the storm clouds hanging low over the oily water. Silence lay over the marina, broken only by the moan of the wind as it played through the stainless-steel shrouds that braced the sloop's mast.

In the shadowed cabin, a figure stirred. Shapeless in yellow rain gear, it lifted a hand and pushed back the hood that fell half down its face. Dark hair, curling with dampness, fell free. Nicole expelled her breath and wiped the back of her hand across her forehead.

The cabin was airless. That, coupled with the closeness of the rubberised rain gear, had made the past hour seem interminable. She pushed back her sleeve and looked at her watch. Soon, she thought, and a tremor of anticipation raced through her. Chase Tarrant would board his boat, he would call to his crewman to cast off—and then it would all be up to her.

The waiting was the worst part; it was like sitting outside the headmistress's office for your part in a prank gone wrong. The reality of the confrontation was never as bad as you expected.

That she'd even come this far was something of a miracle. There'd been so little time to set things into motion—the plan that had brought her here had only crystallised a few hours earlier. After the terrible scene at

the yacht club, standing beside Aston in the chill night air
outside the clubhouse, Nicole had been so filled with rage
that she couldn't think at all. She'd only been half
listening, and when Aston had put his arm around her
shouders and begun leading her towards the door, she'd
balked.

'What are you doing?' she'd demanded.

'We have to go back to the party, Nicki.'

She'd twisted free of his arm. 'I am not going back into
that room, Aston. I never want to see those people again.
How can you even ask . . .'

'Nicki, listen to me. If we go inside now, we can turn
what happened against Tarrant. We'll say he was drunk,
we'll laugh it off and . . .'

Nicole spun towards him. 'You laugh it off, dammit! I
can't.'

Aston flushed. 'I told you, I'll have the last laugh.'

'When?' she demanded. 'When, Aston? You've had
half a dozen opportunities and you've let them all slip by.'

His eyes narrowed. 'What are you suggesting, Nicki?
Should I have challenged him to a duel?' He laughed
bitterly. 'He would probably have taken me up on it.'

'No,' she said quickly, 'no, of course not. I . . . I didn't
mean . . .'

Aston pulled out his cigarette case and lit up. 'There are
other ways to handle someone like Tarrant. I don't have to
descend to his level.' He looked at her through a cloud of
smoke. 'Trust me, Nicki. This race will teach the man a
lesson he'll never forget.'

'He'll probably win it,' Nicole said flatly. 'What kind of
lesson will that be, Aston?'

'He won't win. He won't even be a contender.'

Her eyebrows rose. 'What's in that cigarette you're
smoking, Aston? You commissioned the boat he's going
to sail, remember? It has an advanced hull design, the

latest computer gadgetry . . .' She laughed bitterly. 'He's probably got Dennis Connor crewing for him.'

Aston didn't laugh. 'He's got some red-headed kid. Billy Essex, I think his name is. Not that it matters.'

Nicole sighed. He was right, it didn't matter, but not for the reason Aston thought. He could say what he liked: she knew that Tarrant would win the race. She could feel it in her bones. Only a miracle would stop him. Or an act of God. Or . . .

Sabotage. The thought came to her with a swiftness that stole her breath away. Sabotage. A broken instrument. Lost charts. Fouled drinking water. Something, anything that would destroy his chances of winning.

Yes, it would be so simple! She glanced at Aston. He was talking to her, his voice low and soothing, and she nodded and smiled and let him take her elbow and lead her back to the clubhouse. Sabotage, she thought. The word had the sound of silk.

Enchantress was moored not five minutes' walk from here. It would be easy enough to slip on board and toss an electronic gadget overboard and watch it sink beneath the dark water.

Elation fled as quickly as it had come. It would be an exercise in futility. Tarrant would discover the loss the next morning and replace whatever she'd tossed away before he set sail. She might delay him an hour or two, but that was meaningless in a race this long.

No, she thought as Aston pushed open the door to the clubhouse, no, if you were going to stop a man like Tarrant, you'd have to do something clever. You'd have to destroy some vital part after he was so far at sea that he'd be forced to limp home in defeat. And that would be impossible. No one but Chase and his crewman would have access to *Enchantress* once the boat left the marina.

'That's my girl,' Aston whispered, putting his arm

around her shoulders.

Nicole looked at him in surprise. She hadn't even realised that they were back inside the clubhouse until he'd spoken; he was smiling at her, and she managed to smile back at him as his friends gathered around them. Aston began making jokes about 'upstarts' and men who couldn't hold their drink, and his friends laughed. But she noticed that no one spoke to her. The women stared at her with strange, glistening eyes, as if they had a thousand questions they feared to ask. And the men seemed to avoid her, almost as if Chase's kiss had left a brand on her. After a while, she slipped, unnoticed, to the edge of the circle and moved away.

She was tired. Very tired. Even the game she'd been playing minutes before, the game of thinking of a way to sabotage *Enchantress,* had lost its charm. And that's all it was, after all. It was just a game . . .

'Hey!'

She stumbled back as someone stepped heavily on her toes. A man—a boy, really—caught her by the shoulders.

'I'm sorry, ma'am,' he stammered. 'Did I hurt you?'

Nicole managed a pained smile. 'That's OK,' she said, hobbling to a chair. 'I'll live.'

The boy hurried to her side. 'I *did* hurt you,' he said, squatting down beside her. 'Maybe I broke your toe or something . . .'

She laughed. 'Really, I'm fine.'

He ran his hand through his hair. Red curls fell across his forehead.

'Are you sure?' he asked.

'Yes,' she said, and her eyes narrowed as she looked at him. 'Are you . . . are you Billy—Billy . . .'

'Essex,' he said eagerly. 'Yes, ma'am, that's me.'

Nicole drew in her breath. Billy Essex. The boy who was crewing for Chase Tarrant tomorrow. Fate had put him in her path. If—*if*—she was really going to sabotage *Enchantress,* meeting him might be just the opportunity she needed.

But she wasn't going to do anything like that. Was she?

'May I get you a drink, Miss . . . Miss . . .'

'Wheeler,' Nicole said softly, and then she smiled. 'Yes, thank you, Billy, that would be very nice.'

The boy snatched up two glasses of champagne. 'Here,' he said, handing one to her. She sipped the wine slowly, watching as he gulped his down. He'd already had too much of the bubbly liquid; his face was flushed, his eyes red-rimmed and shiny. Nicole ran her tongue over her lips.

'Someone told me you were crewing for Mr Tarrant,' she said. 'Is that true?'

The boy nodded. 'Yeah,' he said eagerly, and he launched into a long, slurred speech extolling the wonders of the man she hated. Nicole felt her smile slipping. The half-formed idea that had been in her mind died. Billy clearly idolised Tarrant; he'd never agree to do anything to the man's boat, not even if she smiled and batted her eyelashes all night long.

She sipped her champagne, nodding and smiling, only half listening as the boy talked about the forthcoming race. He was excited about it, he said. He loved sailing, he said. It was just this rotten weather; he hated having to wear all that bulky foul-weather gear and safety harness, but Mr Tarrant would insist. He was a stickler for safety . . .

Nicole felt a prickling sensation along her skin. Foul-weather gear, she thought. Her pulse quickened. *Bulky* foul-weather gear. It was more than bulky. It was shapeless and concealing.

Her eyes flickered over the boy. They were roughly the same height. They were both slight of build. In the bulky rain gear, in the driving rain and wind, who would be able to tell them apart? And the rain was supposed to continue all night and into the next evening.

She swallowed. Was it—was it possible? The boy was already reeling; was there a way to get him even drunker, to tuck him safely away and put herself in his place?

No. It was impossible. She could never do it. She'd have to lead him on, lure him out of here . . .

Billy lurched to his feet. 'I . . . I don't suppose you'd like to come for a walk, would you?' he said.

Nicole was almost afraid to breathe. She looked across the room for Aston, but he'd vanished.

'Yes,' she said quickly, before she lost courage. 'Yes, I would.'

The boy almost tripped over his feet in his rush to get her coat and lead her to the door. It was cold outside. The rain had picked up and was coming down in sheets. Billy took her arm and leaned towards her. Nicole almost gagged from the smell of alcohol on his breath.

'My rooms're just up the street. Wouldja like to come up for a beer?'

Nicole could barely speak. 'Yes,' she whispered. 'Why not?'

Her heart began to pound as they climbed the stairs to his room. What was she doing? What was supposed to happen next? The boy was drunk, but he was still standing. And he wasn't really a boy. He was her age, at least. For all she knew, he always put away this much drink before a race. Maybe it just made his reflexes sharper. Maybe he'd get her to his room and turn into an octopus. Maybe . . .

'There we go,' he said, waving her into a small, dark room. He switched on the lights and grinned lopsidedly. 'Lemme jus' go get us that beer.'

Nicole shook her head. 'I can't do this,' she said. 'Billy, I'm sorry. I . . .'

But he was already staggering away from her. She waited nervously, twisting the belt of her raincoat between her fingers. When he came back, she'd make up some excuse, tell him she had to get back to the clubhouse. Billy wasn't the only one who'd had too much champagne. Apparently she had, too.

Change places with Chase's crewman? Play a dangerous game, alone at sea with a man she feared, so she could commit an act of sabotage against him?

Nicole almost laughed aloud. She hadn't even been able to carry out step one, which was to incapacitate Billy Essex. Where was he, anyway? She frowned and stepped further into the room.

'Billy?' There was no answer. 'Billy? Are you all right?'

Was the boy ill? Guilt washed over her. Suppose he'd passed out? Suppose he'd fallen in the kitchen, hit his head against the floor? Suppose . . .

A loud, rasping noise startled her. Nicole cocked her head and listened as the sound was repeated, and then she walked slowly towards it.

There was a kitchen at one end of the hall and a bedroom at the other. Billy lay sprawled on his back across a rumpled bed, a foolish grin on his face. Nicole stood over him, watching the rise and fall of his chest, and then she touched his arm.

'Billy? Billy, are you OK?'

He mumbled in his sleep, burped gently, and rolled on to his side. As he did, something shiny tumbled from his pocket.

It was a silver disc. The name *Enchantress* was engraved on its face; from it hung what Nicole knew must be the key to the boat's companionway hatch.

She drew in her breath. All right, she thought, it was fate. It was foolish to question it any longer. Carefully, she picked up the key-ring and tucked it into her pocket.

'Thank you, Billy,' she whispered, and she drew the blanket from the foot of the bed and covered the sleeping figure. She started from the room, then turned back and disconnected the alarm clock that stood beside the bed. 'Sleep well,' she said, and shut the door quietly behind her.

Aston was the next problem. She had to find a way to peel him away from his friends. She glanced at her watch as she hurried back towards the marina. It was getting late, and there was still a lot to do. She had to get home, change her clothes . . .

She cried out when a figure stepped out of the shadows and into her path.

'Nicole?'

'Aston!' She put her hand to her throat, wondering if he could see the swift, tell-tale pulse racing beneath her palm. 'Oh, you scared the life out of me!' She laughed nervously. 'I . . . I just stepped out for a breath of . . .'

Aston took her arm. 'I was just going back inside to find you,' he said, hurrying her towards the car park. 'It's time we were going.'

'Yes,' she said with relief, 'I think so, too.'

'It's getting late, and I have to be back here early in the morning.'

In the morning. Sunday morning. Would he expect her to accompany him? 'I don't think I could get up early tomorrow if my life depended on it,' she said quickly. 'I . . . I think I'm coming down with something.'

He nodded as he opened the car door for her. 'Take some aspirin.'

'Right.' She glanced at him from under her lashes as he turned the engine on. 'Maybe I'll unplug my phone and spend the day sleeping.'

To her surprise, he didn't argue. 'Fine, fine. I'll call you tomorrow evening.'

'No,' she said quickly, 'no, don't do that. Let me just

take it easy. I'll see you at the office on Monday.'

'Yes, all right,' he said.

She unclasped the diamond and emerald necklace as he drove and lay it on the console between them. She'd half expected an argument, but Aston only nodded and she breathed a sigh of relief.

His preoccupation with Tarrant was making everything much easier than she'd expected. She wanted to tell him not to worry, that she'd figured out a way to pay the man back. But she kept silent, knowing he'd only try to talk her out of it, and no one was going to do that. Her retaliation might not be as legal as a lawsuit, but it was going to be much more satisfying.

When they reached her apartment building, she bade him a quick goodnight and then hurried inside. As soon as she saw his car pull away, she closed the curtains and stripped off her silk dress and high heels, exchanging them for jeans, a sweatshirt and boat shoes. Then she snatched up her car keys and a flashlight and hurried from her apartment.

The offices of the Powell Corporation were only a ten-minute drive away. Aston owned the whole building, a smoky glass cube near the ocean. There was no security guard, only a coded lock that opened easily when Nicole inserted her employee identification card. Her office was on the first floor, just outside Aston's. She stepped inside, closed the blinds and turned on her desk-lamp. Then she uncapped her pen and pulled a sheet of paper towards her.

'Dear Aston', she wrote, and then stopped and touched the tip of her tongue to her teeth.

How to explain? How could she explain something to Aston that she couldn't explain to herself? She only knew that fortune, fate, whatever, had given her an opportunity and she'd be damned if she passed it by. Well, there was no time to search for all the right words. Short and sweet would have to do. She'd be back before she was even missed. She could explain to Aston then.

The pen flew over the paper. 'Dear Aston, I haven't much time to write this. Chase Tarrant's in for a shock. Someone had to teach him a lesson, a lesson he'll remember as long as he lives, and I wanted to be that someone.'

She signed her name, then read the note aloud. It wasn't enough, but it would do. Hastily, she recapped the pen and tucked the note into the blotter on Aston's desk.

The marina lay silent when finally she reached it. The clubhouse was dark. One or two lights winked far out on the water. Nicole's heart hammered in her chest as she approached *Enchantress's* slip. What if Chase had decided to sleep on board? What if he was already below? What if . . .

Stop it! Are you really going to turn tail and run after all this?

'Yes,' she whispered, swallowing a mouthful of nervous laughter.

But she was already padding silently across the deck. The key she'd taken from Billy Essex fitted the hatch. It opened easily, giving way to yawning darkness. Nicole paused, every sense alert. Then, slowly, she made her way down the ladder.

There was no one on board. She was positive of that; there was an emptiness to the silence that told her so. But her pulse raced as she switched on her flashlight and aimed its narrow beam around the dark cabin. To her left, there was a galley, complete with small refrigerator, sink, and stove. Behind it there was a quarter berth for sleeping or storage. Someone had loaded it with canvas sailbags and cardboard boxes.

Nicole swung the light to her right. The beam played over a large navigation desk and chart cabinet. She saw a radio set into a shelf in the cabin wall beside it, but the purpose of the computer display screens, multi-position switches, and assorted electronic gauges was unknown to her.

Aston's designs. The thought gave her courage.

She moved forwards slowly. There was a large table offset to the left, flanked on three sides by a wrap-around couch. Another couch faced it on the other side of a narrow walkway. Beyond the forward bulkhead there was a compact head, complete with toilet, sink, and shower. There was a large storage locker opposite. Nicole swung the flashlight all the way forwards. There was another berth in the bow of the boat. It was empty.

'OK.'

She spoke the word aloud, deliberately using her voice to make the strange, shadowy space familiar. She took a breath, then another. So far, so good. She could feel the tension singing through her blood, but it gave her the courage to continue. She had the feeling it was only adrenalin that was keeping her knees from buckling.

The flashlight beam flickered. The batteries—lord, she had no idea how old they might be! What she had to do must be done quickly, before the light gave out and she was trapped in the dark, waiting for Chase Tarrant to board his boat and find her.

The thought set her heart to hammering. Don't think about that, she urged herself. Just get to work.

The foul-weather gear. Where was the damned stuff? It had to be here—Aston kept his stowed on his boat. That was where everybody kept it, wasn't it? Her mouth turned dry as she poked into the nearest locker. If she didn't find the rain gear, the game was over before it began.

But it was there, in the locker by the companionway steps, hanging neatly and waiting. Nicole had put the flashlight on the table and then pulled the waterproof clothing on over her jeans and sweatshirt. Her hands had trembled, but she had dutifully zipped the zippers and snapped the snaps, and then she'd looked around the cabin, finally deciding to tuck herself into the head.

And that was where she'd been for heaven only knew how long now, sitting patiently on the closed toilet seat, waiting for Chase. Nicole frowned and pushed back her sleeve. Why wasn't he here yet? The race began soon—it was past dawn. Watery light streamed into the cabin. Rain still pattered on the deck, but it sounded as if the worst was over. She could hear the marina stirring around her, hear the calls of the ever-present gulls and the voices of captains and their crewmen as they talked to each other.

As they talked to each other!

Nicole sprang to her feet. How could she have been so stupid? From a distance, she might pass for Chase's crewman in this outfit. But she'd never sound like him; even if she pitched her voice as low as she could, he'd hear the difference, he'd know, he'd realise what she'd done. Her pulse raced crazily. Insanity, that was what it was, to think she could get away with something like this.

She thought of his savagery that day in Aston's office, of the shackled power she'd felt in him each time he'd forced her into his arms.

Her heart leaped to her throat in terror and she began to tremble. She had to get off this boat. Quickly, before anyone saw her, before Chase found her. Nicole snatched her flashlight and tucked it into her pocket. No, she thought, not her pocket. It was Billy's pocket. She had to peel off this damned rain suit and put it away and . . .

'No!'

The whispered cry was wrenched from her throat. She put her hand to her mouth, trying to stifle the sound of her own breathing. Footsteps moved across the deck above, footsteps that were firm and purposeful. She shrank back into the shadows, into the narrow confines of the head.

'Billy? Are you down there, boy?'

It was Chase's voice. The blood drained from her face. Her hands trembled as she pulled the hood up over her head, then tugged it down on her forehead.

'Billy?'

Feet thudded on the rungs of the ladder. Nicole put her hand to her breast, as if to try and keep her heart from flying out from between her ribs. He was in the cabin; she could hear him walking towards her. Desperately, she turned away, flipped the bathroom bowl open, and bent over it.

'Hey, kid, what's the matter? Are you sick?'

She nodded. The footsteps paused behind her, and she felt the light touch of a hand on her back.

'Dammit, Billy, didn't I tell you not to drink too much? You know you can't hold liquor worth a damn.'

Nicole shrugged her shoulders. 'Unh,' she rasped.

'Will you be OK?'

She was almost afraid to breathe. 'Unh huh.'

'Splash some cold water on your face and then make us some coffee. I'll go topside and get the boat ready.' He slapped her on the back, and it was all she could do not to fall into the bowl. 'Dammit, kid, if I didn't need you, if I thought I could get somebody else at this hour, I'd kick your drunken ass over the side so fast . . .' There was a silence, and then Chase sighed. 'Oh, what the hell?' he said. 'It's not as if I haven't worshipped at that altar once or twice in my time. But if you're not on deck in fifteen minutes, you're in for a long swim. Do you hear me?'

She heard the clang of the locker and she peered cautiously over her shoulder. Chase's back was to her; he was wearing a faded chambray shirt, taut across his broad shoulders and back, and a pair of jeans. She watched as he slipped into coveralls and a slicker that matched her own.

He was half-way to the deck when he paused and looked back at her.

'Billy?'

She shuffled forwards a couple of steps, then stopped. 'Unh?' she said, looking at him from under the shadow of her hood.

Chase grinned, the flash of his teeth very white against his tanned skin. A gust of wind ruffled his hair, tossing it across his forehead.

'We're going to win this race in record time,' he said. 'I want to get back to Coral City fast. I've got something very important to take care of.' He laughed softly. 'Understand?'

Nicole nodded and raised her hand in salute. She watched as Chase turned and scrambled on to the deck, and then she let out her breath.

Something very important.

Some politician to bribe, probably. Some contract to steal. Honestly, the arrogance of the man! As far as he was concerned, he'd already crossed the finish-line and collected his trophy. He couldn't imagine that he might lose.

But he would. Nicole looked up at the deck as Chase's shadow moved past the cabin door. A swift, fierce sense of joy sent her heart racing, banishing the fear that had almost sent her running into the rainy morning moments before.

She was still frightened, yes. She had trapped herself in a corner with a violent, dangerous man. But that didn't matter.

Chase Tarrant would lose, and she would be the instrument of his defeat. What could be more important than that?

CHAPTER FIVE

THERE was a percolator in a locker in the galley, and a jar of coffee in the fridge. Nicole filled the pot and set it on the stove. When it was ready, she filled two heavy white mugs, picked them up, and then set them down again.

Did Tarrant take his coffee black? With cream? Or with sugar? She stared at the steaming mugs and frowned. Surely Billy Essex would know something so basic about the man he'd sailed with before? Well, she thought, there was no way around it. She'd have to take a tray on deck with her. Pretending she was suffering a hangover had got her over the rough spots so far—she'd just have to hope it worked again.

He was at the wheel when she came topside. Carefully, she set the tray down next to him. Then she picked up a mug and moved quickly to the lee side of the boat.

Chase looked at the cream pitcher and sugar bowl and shook his head. 'Boy, you really must have tied one on last night, kid,' he said, picking up his mug and enfolding it in his hands. 'Since when do I take my coffee any way but black and hot?'

Nicole froze for a second. She looked at him and he grinned, and she let out her breath and managed a wheezy laugh. Letting Chase think 'Billy' was hungover was turning out to be an unplanned touch of genius. The hangover, combined with the rain and the wind, would give her all the safety she needed until she'd accomplished what she'd set out to do.

Just you wait, she thought with grim satisfaction, just

you wait, Mr Tarrant. I'm going to make you sorry you ever tangled with me . . .

Chase put down the mug and gestured impatiently. 'Come on, kid, are you going to stand around and stare at me all day? There's a lot to do before we cast off.' She said nothing, and he sighed. 'How many brain cells did you kill off last night, Essex? Try hoisting the burgee, for starters.' His eyebrows rose. 'You can manage that, can't you?'

Nicole swallowed hard. 'Yeah,' she rasped gruffly, and she turned away from his sarcastic smile.

Hoist the burgee. Sure, she could do that. The burgee was a swallow-tailed flag at the masthead; it carried the club's colours. Aston had shown her how to attach it to the flag-hoist with a knot called a clove hitch.

The knot was a simple one, really. But not when you were wearing gloves, and she had to keep them on. If Chase saw her hands, half the size of a man's and uncallused as well, the game would be over before it began. Nicole's tongue pushed between her teeth as she fumbled at the rope for a third time.

There! That had done it. She smiled to herself as she hoisted the flag and watched it flap in the wind.

'Clear the mainsail.'

Her head sprang up at the sound of Tarrant's voice. Nicole looked at him, then at the length of furled sail that lay along the boom. The last time she'd uncovered the mainsail on *Fortune's Fancy,* Aston had teased her about the messy way she'd folded and stowed the cover. Not that it mattered: Aston always paid a couple of the boys who worked at the yacht club to put the boat in order after they docked. The kids would re-do any job that hadn't been done well. Nicole looked up and glanced at Chase. He was doing something with the furled jib, and she had the sudden, definite feeling that he wouldn't laugh off a job done poorly.

'Come on Essex, we haven't got all day.'

His voice flayed her like a whip. Wait until tomorrow, she told herself, and the thought got her through the endless chores he assigned. At least none of them was complicated—she could see that Tarrant was the kind of man who preferred doing the difficult things himself. Every now and then, Nicole had to hurry over what she was doing so she could move off and keep some distance between them.

She breathed easier when the rain picked up. It slanted down in grey sheets, clearing the docks of the few people who'd braved the morning to see the boats off. Nicole tugged her hood down until it was almost resting on the bridge of her nose, and risked a glance at Chase. He'd done the same, and she smiled to herself. No one would ever be able to tell who was tucked away in one of these rain suits.

His voice cut through her musing. 'All right, kid. Let's get to it. Cast off the bow line.'

She nodded and hurried forwards. This was the first drill she'd mastered under Aston's tutelage, and she could do it with her eyes closed. Slip the line free, then haul it in. Then bring in the fender. When Tarrant barked out the order for the stern line, she was there before the words were out of his mouth. By the time she'd finished coiling both the mooring lines and stowing them away, *Enchantress* was motoring slowly up the channel.

Nicole stood on the forward deck, huddled in her rain gear, and watched Chase at the wheel. He was a study in concentration, looking first at the marker buoys in the narrow channel, then peering ahead through the rain, eyes narrowed against the wind.

He shoved his hood back and it slipped to his shoulders. Rain glistened in his hair, and the wind blew it in dark tangles across his forehead. He thrust his hand into it impatiently and brushed it back from his face. He looked, Nicole thought suddenly, like a man from another century, a man born to the sea and the ships that once sailed it. In some other life, the burgee flapping wildly at the masthead surely would have carried the white skull and crossbones of the Jolly Roger.

A shudder went through her, as if the wind had pierced her rain gear and clothing and touched a cluster of nerve-endings beneath her skin. What was she doing here? What kind of fool was she to have thought she could play games with a man like Chase Tarrant and come out ahead? If he'd been able to bring Aston to his knees, what might he do to her when he found out . . .?

Stop it. He'll be angry as hell, but there won't be a thing he can do about it. And you'll have won, Nicole, you'll have beaten him.

'Billy.' She looked up, and Chase waved her to the cockpit. 'Go below and make sure everything's stowed away. We're going to hit some rough water when we get outside the harbour—I don't want things getting smashed about in the cabin.'

She nodded. Rain beat into her face as she moved past him to the companionway and the wind plucked at her, sneaking under her slicker until it flapped crazily around her. She scrambled down the ladder into the cabin, sighing with relief to be sheltered from the storm.

Rougher water than this? No, he couldn't have said that. She must have misunderstood. What he'd meant was that it would *seem* rougher, once they were on the open sea. But that was all right. If it weren't that she was tense with the fear of discovery most of the time, she might almost be enjoying herself.

Aston would say she was crazy, but there was something exciting about the keening moan of the wind and the drill of the rain. She thought of Chase in the cockpit, his powerful hands spread on the wheel, his face turned to the sky, and a shudder danced along her skin.

She shook her head. There was work to be done, and she'd better get to it. She stowed away the few things she found lying loose, then checked the storage lockers and closed them. Finally, she took care of the galley, whistling softly through her teeth as she washed out the mugs and the percolator and then put them away.

The cabin was neat enough—what would Billy do next? Start lunch, probably. Soup, she thought, staring into the locker above the sink. Soup and crackers. And for dinner, she'd open one of the freeze-dried packages neatly lined on the shelf. Chilli, maybe. Or stew. She nodded thoughtfully. Something like that, something she could spoon into mugs. Chase could have his topside while she ate in the galley. Maybe she could make her move then, before the weather cleared.

The only question was, what move would it be? She looked around her again. *Enchantress* was filled with gadgets. But which were vital? Surely, some duplicated the work of others. And some, if broken, could be repaired on board or done without or . . .

'Billy!'

Something banged heavily above her head. The towel fell from her hands and she zipped up the slicker and tugged at her hood. She didn't need a crystal ball to know that Tarrant was stamping his foot on the teakwood deck.

She clung to the ladder as she scrambled on deck. The boat was pitching wildly and she was surprised to see that they were almost out of the harbour. The shoreline was a dark smear through the sheeting rain, but not as dark as Chase's angry face.

'What the hell were you doing down there, Essex? Sleeping it off?'

Nicole shook her head. 'Uh-uh.'

His expression grew colder. 'I'm tired of playing charades, boy. You'd better find your tongue and find it fast.' He glared at her and then motioned her to his side. 'Take the helm.'

She looked at him. 'What?' she asked hoarsely.

'Take the wheel,' he repeated irritably. 'We're coming up on the marker buoy. I have to go below and radio the race committee.' His teeth flashed in a quick grin. 'Then we'll raise these sails and ride the wind.'

The deck dipped beneath her feet as she made her way to him, and the water seemed to rise towards her, a glassy grey-green frothed with white. Her stomach made a first, almost delicate move, lifting to a point somewhere just behind her breastbone before gently falling back to where it belonged. Saliva filled her mouth, and she swallowed.

'Hold her steady on a heading of a hundred and sixty-five degrees,' he shouted. 'Remember, give us plenty of sea-room when you pass the Dragon's Teeth beacon.'

She nodded as his hands slid from the wheel. The Dragon's Teeth—she'd need no warning buoy to remind her of their presence. But this was nothing like sailing past the Teeth—a boat under motor power was simple to steer, even in this weather. What would *Enchantress* be like once they reached the head of the channel and Chase put her under sail?

She was so intent on following the compass heading that she jumped when his hand closed on her shoulder.

'OK, kid. I'll take her. Stand by to hoist the mainsail.'

Nicole made her way carefully along the windward side of the boat to the mainmast boom. She could handle this, too. The first step was to free the shock cords that held the furled sail. She fumbled at one, then another.

'Come on, Billy, let's go, let's go!'

Chase's voice was sharp with impatience. She knew she was taking too long, but she couldn't help it. Billy's gloves were at least two sizes too big, but she couldn't take them off . . .

'Come *on!* I want that sail up, pronto!'

There was no time to waste. Nicole put one hand to her mouth. Her teeth closed around the glove and she yanked it off, then jammed it into her pocket. After a minute, she grinned to herself and raised her gloved hand in salute.

'OK. Stand by the mainsail halyard.'

She edged back to the cockpit, careful of her footing and handholds as the sloop rose and fell with the waves. Her stomach shifted uneasily, but she swallowed hard and that seemed to do the trick. Grunting, Nicole coiled the rope that would raise the sail around the winch.

'OK. Hoist away, Billy.'

She nodded, took a deep breath, and grasped the winch handle. The sail moved a couple of feet up the mast, then stopped. Nicole drew in her breath, then cranked the handle again.

Chase muttered an oath. 'Come on, dammit, put your back into it.'

She bit down on her bottom lip. Her back? Her back was already in it, damn the man! And her arms and her shoulders, too.

But she couldn't tell him that. She could only urge the sail up the mast while the boat pitched and rolled beneath her, until finally it was billowing in the gusting wind.

'The luff, Essex! Secure the mainsail halyard and take the slack out of the luff!'

The luff? What in heaven's name was the luff? *The leading edge of the sail.* Captain Bligh wanted her to tighten the downhaul line and stop the sail edge from shaking in the wind. She wanted to scream back at him, to tell him to try speaking English. Instead, she did as he'd ordered—but not quickly enough, apparently. She could hear his curses over the increasing shriek of the wind.

'What the hell's wrong with you, Essex?'

For a second, she almost told him.

I'm not Essex, she wanted to yell. But she didn't. She turned away when Chase glared at her, and grasped the rope guardrail tightly as *Enchantress* lurched and bucked her way into the open sea.

It was never going to work. She knew it now; she could never make Chase Tarrant think she was Billy Essex, not once they were under sail. She didn't have the skill nor the strength nor the experience. He would see through her faster than you could see through a pane of glass, long before she'd had time to even think of what to sabotage, and then . . .

With terrifying swiftness, *Enchantress* reared against a white-frothed wave, shuddering at its touch as a wild horse might at the brush of a saddle. Nicole cried out, stumbled against Chase, then grabbed wildly at the rail again. When she looked out to sea, her heart seemed to stop beating.

Large, white-capped waves rolled across the green-grey ocean. The wind howled from a charcoal sky, pawing at the boat like a cat with a mouse. Nicole's stomach turned over. Eyes wide, she turned to Chase, waiting for him to say they would have to run for shore.

What she saw made her blood run cold. His face was turned to the wind, a look of such joy and excitement on it that she felt, for a moment, that she'd intruded upon something very private. It was clear he was having the time of his life.

Her stomach rose rapidly from somewhere behind her navel to a point mid-way up her throat. Saliva rolled into her mouth. She swallowed rapidly, then swallowed again.

'Force six winds,' Chase yelled. She stared at him from under the overhanging hood. 'Force six and building! Damn,' he said, and he threw back his head and laughed. 'We'll give those mothers a run for their money.'

Nicole swallowed again. 'Uh,' she said, 'unh . . .'

There was barely time to clap her hand to her mouth, turn to the rail, and bend across it. She gagged once, and then the black coffee she'd drunk earlier rushed to join the churning ocean.

'What the . . .? Are you crazy, Essex? You . . .'

Nicole gagged again as another wrenching spasm shook her body. She groaned, closing her eyes against the foam-flecked waves rising towards her.

'What are you trying to do? The last thing we need right now is a man overboard drill.' Chase's voice was thick with anger and sarcasm. 'Hang on tight, Essex. I want the pleasure of drowning you myself.'

But Nicole was past listening. She moaned as the boat rose up and then fell heavily into a trough. Terrible things were happening in her belly, and she wrapped her arms around her middle and bent over as if that might stop them.

'Damn you, Essex. If I had a bottle of champagne handy, I'd take it and ram it . . .'

Nicole groaned and stumbed against the railing. Chase cursed and grabbed her, curving his arm around her waist, holding her to him in a tight, impersonal grasp.

'Lean on me,' he said. 'Come on, boy. I'll hold you up.'

It was as if time were flowing backwards. This was how it had been the day they met, Nicole thought hazily. She'd been sick and shaking, and Chase had taken her in his arms, letting her draw her strength from him. She wanted to turn into his embrace, bury her face against the curve of his shoulder, burrow against him and seek the solace his arms had once offered.

But she couldn't. She couldn't! What was wrong with her? He was Chase Tarrant, her enemy. And she—she wasn't even Nicole Wheeler, she was Billy Essex, she was his crewman . . .

Nicole fought free of his arm. 'Going below,' she gasped in a hoarse whisper. 'I . . .'

She stumbled as *Enchantress* rose and fell again, and Chase reached out for her.

'Easy,' he said, 'it's OK, I've got you.'

The deck tilted and she sagged against him. There was the quick press of his chest against her breasts, the quick feel of his hands moulding the curve of her hips, and then she shoved him from her.

Chase looked at her. 'Billy?'

Nicole put her hand to her mouth and pushed past him. In a desperate rush, she half tumbled down the companionway into the cabin, then raced for the head, lifted the bowl cover, and bent over it.

A long time later, she made her way to the main berth. She was trembling with exhaustion, but at least she felt more like living than dying. Carefully, she sat down and put her hands to her face.

How long had she been in the cabin? It seemed like hours. First she'd been too ill to move and then, after she'd found the bottle of dramamine in the medicine locker and downed three of the little tablets, after they'd taken her from violent nausea to queasiness, she'd been too frightened to move, sure that even walking would set her stomach adrift again.

She sighed and fell back on the berth. What a close call that had been on deck. Another few seconds and Tarrant would surely have realised the 'boy' he held in his arms wasn't a boy at all. Actually, for a minute there, she'd thought . . .

Nicole closed her eyes wearily. Her imagination always got the best of her when she was ill, she thought drowsily. Her mother used to tease her about it when she was little. There was the time she'd run a high fever and she'd seen elephants in the corner of her bedroom. And the time

she'd had the measles and she'd been certain her Raggedy
Ann doll was . . . was . . .

*She was adrift on a glassy sea. The sun was bright, the
water warm, and she was sprawled on the deck of a
sailing-boat, face and body turned to the sun. A man
dropped down beside her, a man with cool, grey eyes and a
smiling mouth. 'There you are,' he whispered. 'I was
afraid I'd lost you . . .'*

'There you are. I was afraid you'd tried flushing
yourself down the toilet.'

Nicole gasped and sprang up in the berth. The cabin was
dark; only faint light from the portholes illuminated it.
Quickly, she pulled up her hood and stared towards the
companionway. Chase was silhouetted against the hatch.
She couldn't see his face, only his wide shoulders and long,
lean body. His legs were crossed at the ankles, his arms
over his chest.

He laughed softly. 'Cat's still got your tongue, hey?'
She shrank back as he moved further into the cabin and
bent towards the navigation desk. She heard a click, and
then a light flared. 'That's one hell of a hangover you've
got, kid.' He straightened up and the light cast an eerie
glow across his eyes and cheekbones. 'I've never heard of
champagne leaving a man mute.'

Nicole swallowed nervously. Why was he looking at her
that way? His eyes were narrowed, almost gleaming with
sardonic amusement. She wondered how long she'd been
asleep. Five minutes? Ten? An hour? Had he—had he
been watching her all that time?

He cocked his head to the side. 'You are feeling better,
aren't you?'

Nicole swallowed. 'Uh-huh,' she whispered.

He grinned. 'Good. Each time I checked, you were still
locked inside the toilet. I was getting ready to break the
door down—but then I came below a while ago and found

you sleeping like a baby.' His voice grew soft. 'Is my bed comfortable, Billy? Is that why you chose it instead of your own?'

Nicole's heart began to race. He knew something. He did. She could hear it, she could feel it, she . . .

Chase moved forwards. In the soft light of the single lamp, she could see him clearly. He'd taken off his heavy rain gear and was dressed in jeans and a dark sweater.

'I see you took some dramamine.' She nodded slowly and he laughed. 'Hey, kid, you should have told me you suffered from motion sickness. I'd have suggested you take those tablets before we even left the marina.'

Nicole swallowed drily. Billy Essex, seasick? No, no, Chase wouldn't have a crewman who got seasick. She knew that . . .

He walked the last few feet towards her, smiled, and reached to her lap. She looked down, horror rushing through her as his hand closed around hers, around her *bare* hand, the one without the glove, the one that was obviously a woman's . . .

'No,' she said, her voice clear and precise, and Chase laughed as his fingers cut into her wrist.

'Yes,' he said, drawing her to her feet. 'I have the other glove, "Billy".' His voice twisted across the name. 'I found it on deck. Come on, Essex,' he said as she gritted her teeth and pulled against him, 'don't be like that. You don't need that glove now.' She winced as he twisted her arm behind her. All the laughter had fled his eyes; they were cold, winter-grey and empty. 'Hell, it's warm as an oven down here.' His teeth flashed in a quick, terrible smile. 'In fact, I think you ought to take this rain gear off.'

'No. No!'

'It's all right, kid.' Chase's voice was soft and soothing. He grasped the zipper to her slicker with his free hand and she struck out at him. He laughed and let go of her wrist, but it was only for a second, only so he could capture both her wrists in his hand and immobilise them. 'Don't worry about a thing. The wind's died down and the rain's let up. We're on self-steering.' His lips drew back from his teeth. 'So why don't you get out of all this wet stuff, and . . .'

Nicole struggled fiercely as the zipper slid open. 'You bastard,' she said. 'You son of a . . .'

He laughed. 'What's the matter, Essex? Don't tell me you've decided to be modest. Hell, you know there's no call for modesty here.' The zipper hissed as it came apart and her slicker fell open. 'Anyway, it's too late for that. We've sailed together too often—I've seen every freckle on your . . .'

She was panting with exertion, making little noises as she twisted and pulled against him, but all she succeeded in doing was bringing her body closer to his.

'Damn you to hell, Chase Tarrant!'

She cried out as his hand moved lightly over her breasts, gently cupping their fullness through her sweatshirt.

'Hey, Bill,' he said with wide-eyed innocence, 'when did that happen?'

'I'll kill you,' she said wildly. 'I swear, I'll . . .'

'And you're not mute after all,' he said, his voice a silken purr. 'Isn't that nice?'

Tears of anger and frustration rose in her eyes. 'How long have you known?'

His eyes were cold on hers. 'Not long enough, Miss Wheeler. I should have figured it out hours ago. Billy's never been half as inept—or half as drunk.' His eyes moved over her, lingering on her breasts as he mentally stripped away her clothing. 'But who the hell expected you to pull a damn-fool stunt like this one?'

Nicole ran her tongue over her lips. 'Wh . . . what are you going to do?'

His eyes narrowed. 'I'm the one asking the questions. I

want to know what you're doing here. Did Powell send you?'

'No. Of course not.'

'He did, didn't he? What was the plan, Nicole? Were you supposed to sabotage the boat?' He tightened his grasp on her wrists and she moaned. 'Did I show up before you'd done the job?'

'That's crazy . . .'

'Are you saying that nobody knows you're here?'

His voice was soft, his questions chilling. If he thought that—if he thought no one could trace her to *Enchantress* . . .

'Aston knows,' she blurted.

Chase laughed. 'Which is it, lady? Did Powell send you or didn't he? It would be just like him to have someone else do his dirty work.'

Nicole shook her head. 'You . . . you don't understand. I . . . I . . .' She gasped as he drew her closer.

'I want the truth.'

The truth? The truth, she thought, staring into Chase Tarrant's hard eyes, was that he was a man capable of anything. There had to be a way to protect herself from him.

'All right,' she said, 'Aston . . . Aston knows. He . . . he didn't want me to. But . . .'

His voice cut across hers. 'Why?' She said nothing, and the pressure on her wrists increased until she felt as if the bones were going to snap. 'Tell me,' he growled.

'Because . . . because *Enchantress* is Aston's boat, not yours. And . . . and I knew how badly he wanted to sail her. And . . . and I thought, if I could at least be part of this race, if I . . . if I could be on the boat when it—when it set sail . . .'

The lie fell into the silence of the cabin. Chase stared at her while her heart raced and raced, and then he smiled.

'You sneaked on board to sabotage my boat.'

Nicole shook her head. 'No. No, of course not. I . . .'

'But I caught you before you had the chance. Don't bother denying it.'

She drew a breath. 'What are you going to do with me?'

Chase laughed. 'I'll bet that's not what you asked Powell when he hung that necklace around your neck.'

'Mr Tarrant . . .'

'Get that rain gear off.'

'I will. If you'll just . . .'

'Now. Get it off now.'

Her head came up and their eyes met. What she saw in his made her tremble. Slowly, Nicole shrugged free of the slicker, then unsnapped the trousers. They fell down her legs and she stepped free of them. Chase kicked them aside and his eyes travelled over her, moving slowly across her breasts as they rose and fell beneath her sweatshirt, then skimming down the long length of her denim-clad legs. She felt naked, despite her clothing.

'Look here,' she said in a shaky whisper, 'you can't just . . .'

His hands shot out and curled around her shoulders. 'Listen,' he said, his voice as cold and sharp as the blade of a knife, 'listen and get this straight. You're an intruder. A trespasser. Heaven only knows what you did to Billy . . .'

'He's fine. He . . . he just had too much to drink. He . . .'

His eyes moved swiftly over her face. 'The fact is, you're here. And you're very definitely unwanted.'

'Isn't that too bad?' she said with more coolness than she felt.

His mouth twisted. 'Damned right, it is. Putting you ashore will mean I've lost the race. I could never make up the time I'd lose.'

Was it really that simple? Her eyes met his; for a

moment she felt a chill of fear at what she saw, but then it was gone, swept aside by a sense of elation. Of course it was that simple! Why hadn't she seen it all along? All the time she'd agonised over how to sabotage his boat, the answer had been right before her eyes. *She* was the disabling factor; Tarrant would be out of the race the minute he turned and made for land.

'Which is why I'm not going to do it.'

'What?' Nicole looked at him. 'What did you say?'

Chase's hands moved slowly on her shoulders. 'I said,' he repeated softly, 'I'm not putting you ashore.'

Her pulse tripped erratically. 'You mean—you'll call the coastguard and have them pick me up?'

'No coastguard.'

Nicole brought her hands up and put them against his chest. She could feel the racing beat of his heart beneath her palms.

'I don't understand.'

'It's not very complicated,' he said softly. 'If I run for shore I'll lose time, and if I ask the coastguard to take you off I'll have to sail *Enchantress* myself. The rules allow a crewman to leave a boat—hell, someone can get sick out here—but you can't replace him.' His eyes moved over her, finally returning with slow insolence to her face. 'Or her.'

Nicole swallowed. 'Yes, but . . .'

'I can't possibly win this race alone, Nicole. I need someone to stand watch, to prepare meals . . .'

A chill threaded through her blood. 'No,' she whispered.

Chase's arms closed around her. 'Yes,' he said, and he smiled. 'It won't be so bad. If you follow orders and do what you're told . . .'

'You . . . you can't be serious. I . . .'

Suddenly, his eyes were as cold as ice on a winter pond.

'I'm deadly serious.'

'No!' Somehow, she managed a quick, nervous laugh. 'You can't . . . you can't force me to . . .'

'I can do whatever I please. I own you.'

Nicole slammed her hands against his chest. 'You're crazy. You can't own another person. You . . .'

Chase's eyes narrowed. 'I'm the owner and master of this sloop. That makes me the only law around.' His arms fell to his sides. 'You're on my boat, against my wishes. You got my crewman drunk just to get here. No, lady, you're very wrong. You *can* own someone—and I own you.'

She stared at him in disbelief. 'No,' she said finally, and then she lifted her chin. 'No,' she repeated, and she whirled towards the navigation desk. The computer screens and electronic boxes might represent a technology she barely understood, but a radio was simple enough to operate. All she had to do was grab the microphone and . . .

She cried out as Chase's hand clamped around hers with a force that sent a numbing tingle up her arm. He threw her aside and reached past her. His fingers closed on the microphone, and she watched in horror as he ripped it free of the radio, throwing it to the deck in a tangle of wire.

The rasping sound of his breath filled the cabin. 'Do as you're told and maybe you'll get out of this in one piece. I want a hot meal. And fresh coffee.' His eyes swept over her one last time. 'And then,' he said softly, 'then, we'll see about the sleeping arrangements.' A terrible smile lit his face. 'I have a feeling that's the one place you're going to be a hell of a lot more use than Billy.'

CHAPTER SIX

THE thing that had surprised Nicole most in the last days of her marriage was how small their flat on Chicago's posh Lake Shore Drive had suddenly become.

The walls seemed to close in when you shared space with someone you preferred to avoid. With gallows humour, she'd dubbed the realisation 'Nicole's First Law of Unhappiness' and told herself that the psychology course she'd suffered through in high school hadn't been an entire waste, after all.

There had been so many things that led to the collapse of the marriage. Nicole had known she and Tony were on shaky ground almost as soon as the honeymoon ended. They didn't really know each other very well— they'd only dated for a few months when he'd proposed.

Tony had swept her off her feet. His attraction had been flattering. Successful, aggressive, he'd seemed to need no one but her. Even his shortcomings had seemed challenges. She'd told herself that his curtness was masculine, that his single-mindedness was determination. But the truth was simpler. Her husband was a cold, driven man whose life centred around himself and his career. Eventually, Nicole came to realise that he'd married her because it was an appropriate time in his career for him to take a wife.

'Don't waste my time with those people again,' he snapped after an evening spent with the couple from across the hall. 'We don't move in the same circles.'

'Children?' he said when she mentioned starting a family. 'Children distract you from important things.'

'I don't have to give you explanations, Nicole,' he said coldly when she asked why he came home after midnight so often.

Eventually, she'd discovered the reason. He was sleeping with the widowed but still very influential wife of one of his firm's partners.

But Nicole had still been a long way from divorce. She believed in the vows she'd taken; sometimes, she thought she might have gone on forever, trapped in one useless attempt after another to mend a relationship that had never really existed—if it hadn't been for those shrinking walls.

Tony wasn't home much, he never had been, but when he was there was no way to escape him. Five rooms turned into one small space filled with his cold looks and uncaring voice, until Nicole had felt as trapped as an insect in a collecting jar and just as desperate for air.

Now, standing in *Enchantress's* cabin, remembering that desperation, she almost laughed. Compared to a forty-foot sailing-boat, the apartment she'd shared with Tony was palatial. At least there she'd had doors to close and walls to hide behind. But there was no refuge on the sloop, no way to get away from Chase at all. *Enchantress* was a self-contained capsule sailing across a universe of empty sea.

Coffee, Chase had said. And lunch. Nicole made both, bringing them to him on deck, returning to collect the empty dishes when he'd finished. Then she went below again and lost herself in work, rearranging the foodstuffs to suit herself, polishing pans that didn't need polishing, making coffee again—when he demanded it—and bringing another mugful to a glowering, silent Chase Tarrant. The work was mindless, meaningless—but she welcomed it. The last thing she wanted was time to think.

At sundown, she made a meal of freeze-dried stew, buttered bread and tinned pudding and brought it to him. He barely looked at her as she set the tray down beside him in the cockpit.

'Do you want something else?' she asked.

Chase glanced at the food. 'That'll do.'

She gritted her teeth, wanting to tell him the meal was more than he deserved, but she knew it was wiser to say nothing.

'There's a thermos in the galley,' he called as she started below. 'Fill it with coffee and bring it to me.'

'Aye aye, Captain,' she said coldly.

Later, she poured some coffee for herself and sat sipping it in the galley. The thought of trying to stuff anything solid down her throat made her nauseous. It wasn't seasickness—that was long gone. It was the thought of what lay ahead, not just the days between *Enchantress's* present position and Barbados, but the nights and what he'd said about them.

When he finally clambered down the ladder to the cabin an hour or two later, Nicole's heart turned over. She was seated at the table in the galley, her face buried in a paperback novel she'd found in the cabin. It was a Western, the kind of thing she never read under the best of circumstances. By now, her brain was hardly working at all. She'd read the opening paragraph four times so far, and she still had no idea what it said.

Nicole stared blindly at the page as Chase walked behind her. The door to the head opened, then shut. When it opened again, minutes later, she was still staring at the same page. The book might have been written in Chinese for all the meaning the words had.

She tensed as Chase passed her. But he said nothing as he headed topside.

Nicole closed the book with trembling hands. There was a strange feeling in the pit of her stomach, a curious mixture of relief and something else, something she shunted quickly to the dark recesses of her tired brain.

Hours passed and he didn't return. She turned on a lamp in the galley, but its light was faint. The darkness and the silence were almost overwhelming, and she began to wonder whether something had happened to Chase. Visions of giant waves and of tilting decks danced through her mind.

'I hope he fell overboard,' she whispered into the silence.

The words were satisfying but not reassuring. If something happened to him, where would that leave her? Alone on the ocean in a boat she couldn't manage, that was where. She rose and walked slowly to the companionway. Maybe—maybe she ought to go on deck and see if everything was all right.

The rain had ended, but there were no stars or moon. Night had closed around *Enchantress* like a giant's fist, squeezing all the light from the world. The only points of visibility were the sloop's running lights, and they did more to emphasise the darkness than to pierce it.

They were moving ahead slowly in a light wind; even so, the sensation of travelling into the unknown was eerie.

'What are you doing on deck?'

She jumped at the sudden sound of Chase's voice. Well, at least he hadn't fallen overboard. She took a step forwards and wrapped her arms around herself. The night was cooler than she'd expected.

'I just thought I'd see if . . . if . . .'

He laughed. 'If I was all right? Such solicitude,

Nicole. I'm touched.'

'Don't be,' she said coldly. 'I was thinking of myself. You ripped out the mike, remember? And you haven't seen fit to show me how any of the other equipment works. If something should happen to you . . .'

'Nothing will.' His voice was flat. 'I'm wearing a life-jacket and a safety harness.'

'I'm delighted to hear that. Now, if you'll excuse me . . .'

'You'll be even more delighted to hear that I'm going to have to spend the night on deck. Visibility's zero, and we're still in the shipping lanes.'

He sounded exhausted. She tried to count the number of hours he'd been at the helm. Twelve? Eighteen? Whatever it was, it was a long time. She blinked as her eyes adjusted to the darkness. Beyond his shoulder, far in the distance, she could just make out what looked like the lighted outline of a Christmas tree.

'Is that a ship?' she asked softly.

Chase nodded. 'Yeah. A freighter—the second in the past hour.' He flexed his shoulders tiredly. 'If one of those mothers runs into us, it's all over.'

How long could one man stay at the helm? If Billy were here, they'd split the watches.

'Are you . . . you must be very tired.'

'Don't worry, Nicole, I'm not going to fall asleep at the wheel.'

She hesitated. 'I could . . .'

Chase laughed. Could what? Have you ever stood watch?'

'Well, no. But . . .'

'Thank you for your generous offer,' he said sarcastically. But I don't much feel like entrusting my life to you just yet.' He shifted his body in the cockpit; for a second, she caught the gleam of the binnacle light reflected in his eyes. 'Go below,' he said wearily. 'One of us might as well get some rest.'

Nicole took a step forwards. 'Don't you think you ought to reconsider? We can still turn back. We . . .'

'I'm in this race to win it, not lose it,' he snapped. 'Now, get below.'

She felt the rush of blood to her cheeks. 'Aye aye, Captain,' she snapped. 'Forgive me for bothering you. Next time, I'll ask permission before I come on deck.'

'That's a terrific idea,' he growled. 'Why don't you remember it?'

She turned sharply and vanished into the companionway. Let him sit at that wheel until he collapses, she thought furiously.

She turned off the galley lamp, threw herself down on the berth opposite the navigation centre, and glared into the darkness. Not that she'd be able to sleep, of course, but she might as well close her eyes for a while . . .

When she opened them again, sunlight was streaming into the cabin. She blinked and rose up on her elbows. He couldn't still be on deck, could he?

Chase came stumbling down the companionway steps just as she swung her legs over the side of the berth. She stared at him as he sank down on the bunk opposite hers. He looked, she thought, like a man who hadn't slept for twenty-four hours, and it occurred to her that that was probably pretty close to accurate. Dark stubble covered his cheeks and chin; his eyes were silver pools in his haggard face.

Had she ever seen anyone look so exhausted? There wouldn't be any harm in offering him some breakfast, would there? She'd do as much for a stray dog . . .

Chase leaned forward. 'I've engaged the self-steerer. The boat's on course and sailing well.' His eyes narrowed. 'You are not to wake me, Nicole. If you do,

you had better be damned sure it's urgent. Is that clear?'
. . . but not a dog that bared its teeth all the time.

The coolness in her voice matched his. 'Perfectly,
Captain. Don't wake you unless it's a typhoon,
submarine attack or sea monsters. Aye aye, sir.'

His eyes fixed on hers. 'If anything happens to my
boat while I'm asleep,' he said in a fatigue-roughened
whisper, 'you will regret it. Do we understand each
other?'

She scrambled to her feet and snapped a salute.
'Completely, Captain. Yes, sir, Captain. I . . .'

But it was a wasted performance. Chase had already
fallen back on the bunk and closed his eyes. His lashes
lay darkly against his cheeks. She stared at him for a
long moment and then turned away.

There was no sense in feeling even the slightest
compassion for a man so desperate to win that he'd do
anything. She, more than anyone, knew that.

She was on deck, sitting cross-legged on the cabin
roof and staring out to sea, when he awoke hours later.
He came through the hatch clutching a reheated cup of
last night's coffee in his hand.

'Anything to report?'

She turned at the unexpected sound of his voice. The
stubble on his face was darker. It made his cheekbones
more prominent, his eyes a paler grey.

'A visitor,' Nicole said sweetly. 'I told him you were
asleep and asked him to please give my regards to the
coastguard.'

Chase took a quick step towards her. He looked so
dangerous that the sarcastic words caught in her throat
like a bone.

'I was kidding,' she said quickly. 'A bird dropped by
for a few minutes.' He said nothing and she smiled
nervously. 'Look, it was only a bad joke. Some kind of

little sea-bird touched down on the mainmast, that's all.'

'I want you to stay out of sight if we should have any visitors,' he said softly.

'Visitors? Out here?' Nicole laughed. 'What are you talking about?'

Chase shrugged as he peered up at the mainsail. 'We're past the major shipping lanes, but we still might spot a boat. If that happens, you're to go below. Do you understand?'

A shadowy fear danced along her spine. 'No,' she said quickly. 'No, I don't. I told you, Aston knows I'm on board. I . . .'

He laughed as he took the helm. 'Your imagination's working overtime, Nicole. Believe me, if I didn't drown you yesterday, I'm not going to. I just want to be sure you don't try and talk your way off my boat. I told you, as far as I'm concerned, you signed on for the voyage. Is that clear?'

Anger stiffened her body as she got to her feet. 'Any other orders?'

'Yes.' His voice was hard as stone. 'I've decided to teach you some basic seamanship. I might as well get some use out of you.'

'Listen here, *Captain* . . .'

'Is that supposed to be an insult?' He smiled coldly. 'Because it isn't, you know. In fact, we'll do just fine if you remember I am, indeed, the captain and master of this boat.'

Her chin rose. 'As if I could forget it,' she said. 'The way you go around barking orders, telling me what to do . . .'

'Despite the best efforts of you and your lover, I'm going to win this race.'

'Leave Aston out of this,' she said quickly. 'He . . .'

'I should have known he'd try something. A man who'd steal another man's boat . . .'

Nicole snorted. 'Aston? *Aston* stole your boat from you? Come on, Captain, I was there, remember? You've got the story backwards. You're the one who did the stealing. You . . .' She winced, her face paling as Chase caught her wrist.

'Listen,' he whispered, 'and listen carefully. Two years ago, your boyfriend and I were in this same race, Coral City to Barbados, and may the best man win.' His face darkened and he pulled her closer to him. 'But the best man didn't win, Nicole. Powell blew out his spinnaker four days out—he should have had the brains to take the sail down when the wind began to pick up. But he was so damned intent on pushing his boat . . .'

Nicole twisted against his hand. 'I don't know what you're talking about. Aston won that race. He told me. He . . .'

'Yes, he won it. He used a private code when he radioed for another sail. A plane dropped it to him, and he went on to win the race.' His lips drew back from his teeth. 'The fact that he'd violated the rules and disqualified himself didn't mean a damn.'

'That's a lie. Aston wouldn't . . .'

'Wouldn't he? I traced down the sailmaker who'd made the spinnaker and the pilot who flew it out to your boyfriend. Powell paid them for their silence and threatened to blacklist them if anything ever got out. They had a living to make . . .' He shrugged. 'I couldn't do anything but plan for this year's race. I hired the best naval architect, I sat with him for hours while we worked up the plans for a forty-foot sloop with a minimum displacement hull, special sails . . .'

Nicole's eyes narrowed. 'The Good Ship Lollipop? Was that . . .?'

He breath hissed as the pressure of his fingers increased. 'The boat I commissioned was *Enchantress*. Oh, she had a different name—but everything else was exactly the same. Powell stole a copy of her plans before her keel had even been laid.'

'Look, this is an interesting story. But . . .'

'This boat is mine, do you understand? Why do you think your boyfriend didn't try and stop me? Why didn't he call the cops or his lawyer or . . .'

'It would have been bad publicity,' Nicole said quickly. 'You knew that. Aston has that new municipal contract.'

Chase's lips drew back from his teeth. 'Indeed he has. And the department head responsible for letting out the contract has a new summer house down in the Keys.'

Nicole wrenched her hand from his. 'Are you suggesting that Aston bribed someone to get that contract?'

'I'm not suggesting anything, Nicole, I'm stating a fact. It's the way Powell does business. He bribes, he pays off, he uses his money to grease his way into every deal he can't get honestly.'

'What incredible nonsense! Aston would never do things like that. He . . .'

'He'd do anything to make sure he wins and I lose.'

'Aston?' She laughed. 'Winning doesn't matter to him. You're the one, Mr Tarrant; you're the man who can't stand losing, who always has to win.'

'That's what life is all about, Nicole—testing yourself against the competition.' His eyes caught hers as he grasped her shoulders. 'But I always play by the rules. There's no point to it otherwise. Anybody can cheat—but only the best win.'

'You make it sound so pure, Mr Tarrant.'

'It is,' he said quickly. 'It can be.'

'And the cost?' Her voice grew bitter. 'Winning always costs something, you know.'

Chase's gaze scanned her face, dropped to her lips and then came to rest on her eyes.

'It all depends on the prize,' he said softly. 'Sometimes, it's worth everything.'

His hands spread on her shoulders, moving lightly along her back. She looked at him, at his narrowed eyes, the pupils dark against the pale grey irises, and her heart tripped erratically.

'Mr Tarrant . . .'

'We're going to spend more than a week on this boat, Nicole.' His voice was soft. 'Just you and me, in a cabin the size of a bedroom.' She felt the heat of his touch through her sweatshirt. 'Don't you think it's time we did away with formality?'

'What I think is that we need some ground rules.' Her voice was breathy, and she cleared her throat. 'I mean, you're right, the cabin isn't very large. And we'll both need privacy. Why don't we agree that I'll have use of the shower and the cabin for the first hour each morning, and then you . . .?'

He smiled at her. 'Such modesty,' he said softly. 'Hell, Billy and I never had a problem.'

His hand was moving lightly along her throat, his fingers warm and rough as they caressed her skin.

Don't let him do this to you. He's just trying to embarrass you. He's done it too many times as it is.

'Nicole.' A slow heat began working its way through her body, spiralling out from the pit of her belly. 'Nicole,' he said again. His voice was husky and soft. 'Do you remember what I said to you that night at the club?'

Remember who this man is. He's a thief. A cheat. And he's just like Tony.

'I want to make love to you, Nicole.' His hands cupped her face and lifted it to his. 'Look at me,' he whispered.

Slowly, her eyes met his. Once, years before, she had gone to an air show and watched as a team of sky-divers stepped from a silver plane and tumbled slowly into the blue. She had wondered what it felt like to fall effortlessly through space that way, wondered if it were as dizzying and exciting as it appeared from the ground.

She knew the answer now. She was falling into Chase's eyes, into those hot, grey pools that burned in his face. She was swaying towards him, her blood thick with anticipation, her body melting as it awaited the touch of his . . .

His breath was warm as he bent towards her. 'Come to the cabin with me, Nicole.'

You despise this man, she told herself frantically.

But the silver promise in his eyes was drawing her under. Look away, she told herself. Look at the sky, at the sea, look anywhere but at him.

A boat. There was a boat out there.

'There's a boat . . .'

She didn't realise she'd said the words aloud until Chase looked over his shoulder and then at her again. His arms tightened around her.

'It's a trawler,' he said impatiently. 'Forget about it.'

Forget it? Forget her one hope of salvation? The fishing-boat was still a dark shape in the distance. Had it spotted them yet? Would it see them at all?

Nicole pushed free of Chase's embrace, scrambled on to the seat in the cockpit, and waved her arms over her head.

'Hey,' she yelled, 'hey, over here!'

In one swift motion, Chase scooped her into his arms and dragged her from the seat.

'Damn you to hell, lady!'

'No,' she cried, 'don't!' Her fists beat against his back as he slung her over his shoulder and stalked to the companionway hatch.

'I warned you,' he said grimly. 'I told you not to try anything like that, didn't I?'

Her head bumped against the hatch cover, her hip banged against something hard and sharp as he carried her down the ladder.

'Put me down. Do you hear me? Damn you, put me . . .'

He did, without ceremony, dumping her on the edge of his berth. His face was as dark as a thunder cloud as he stared at her, and then he turned away and fumbled in one of the storage lockers.

'Hold out your hands.'

His voice was hard, harder than she'd ever imagined it could be. When he turned back to her, the coldness in his eyes took her breath away.

She scrambled to her feet. 'Chase . . .'

'Hold them out, I said.'

She began to tremble. 'I don't understa . . . Chase?' Her voice rose in horror. 'Chase, what are you doing?'

But she could see what he was doing; he was binding her wrists together with a piece of rope, securing it so tightly that she felt it bite into her flesh.

'Please.' Her voice broke. 'Chase, no.'

The bunk hit the back of her knees as he propelled her backwards. She fell on it heavily and he knelt before her and tied her ankles together with a second piece of line.

'Is this all it takes to get you to call me by my first name?' He laughed softly as he lifted her bound ankles and laid her down on the bunk. 'Hell, I would have done it sooner.'

'Chase,' she said, 'listen to me. You don't have to do

this. You . . .'

Her eyes widened in disbelief as he pulled a white handkerchief from his pocket and began to twist it into a narrow strip.

'No, no. Please . . .'

He stuffed the gag between her teeth, muffling her cries.

'Listen to me,' he said.

But his words were meaningless. She was trying to breathe, trying to draw air into her lungs. But she couldn't. She couldn't. Oh, God, she was going to die, to choke . . .

'Nicole!' His voice was as sharp as a gunshot. It tore through the fabric of her terror and she stared up at him. He bent towards her and cradled her face in his hands. 'You're all right,' he said. She swung her head wildly from side to side, and his hands clamped tighter. 'Yes, you are. Breathe slowly. That's it. Again.' He nodded. 'Good girl.'

She told herself it would all be all right, that whatever nightmare she was living would end soon. She felt her racing heart begin to slow. Chase drew back and looked into her face.

'You should have believed me, Nicole. You're staying with me until the end.' He looked into her eyes. 'I'll free you when the trawler's gone. Do you understand?'

Her eyes blazed at him, and she made a sound around the press of the handkerchief.

Damn you! she shouted silently. Damn you and your kind, Chase Tarrant! I'll see you in gaol and throw the key away myself.

His eyes darkened, as if he'd heard the words screaming through her head. Suddenly, he drew in his breath and dropped to his knees beside her. He pulled the rolled handkerchief from between her teeth and bent to her. His mouth was hard on hers, his tongue swift as he thrust it between her lips. Then he drew back, fitted the gag into place again, and hurried from the cabin.

Tears filled Nicole's eyes and flooded down her cheeks.

I hate you, she thought fiercely.

But that wasn't why she was crying.

She was crying because, even now, even after what he'd done to her, Chase's kiss had left her trembling with desire.

CHAPTER SEVEN

NICOLE sighed, closed the book she'd been reading, and let it slip from her fingers. The headache that had plagued her since late afternoon was almost gone, except for an occasional dull throb of pain.

Reading only made it worse. Besides, this was the second time she'd tried to get into the well-thumbed Western, and she still hadn't made any progress. She thought it must be Billy's—she'd seen Chase reading something that looked far more interesting. She'd almost asked if he had other books on board, but then she'd thought better of it. The less she had to do with Chase Tarrant, the better.

There was a sudden pulse-beat of pain at her temples, and she put her hands to her face. If only she'd never boarded *Enchantress*. If only the fishing-trawler had seen her. If only Chase would let her go . . .

'Are you ill?'

She sat up quickly and swung her legs over the side of the bunk. Chase stood at the foot of the companionway ladder, watching her through narrowed eyes.

'If your stomach's feeling queasy, take some dramamine. I don't need you getting seasick again.'

'Your concern is touching, Captain, but . . .'

'My only concern is for this boat. If you're sick, you'll be too busy communing with the bathroom bowl to pull your weight.'

Nicole flushed. 'I've done everything you've requested of me, Captain. If you've any complaints . . .'

Chase gestured impatiently and bent over the navigation desk. 'Look, I haven't the time for this. The wind's building and the seas are running higher. Do us both a favour, Nicole. Take a couple of dramamine tablets.'

She got to her feet. The boat rolled slightly and she grasped the salon table for support.

'You'll be happy to hear my stomach is fine,' she said coldly. 'I won't be communing with the bowl, as you so graciously put it.'

He turned to her. 'Then what is it? You look like hell.'

'Thank you for the compliment, Captain. It's my head. I've got a hell of a pain . . .'

She flinched away as he reached out to her. His fingers touched her face lightly, cool against her cheekbones and eye sockets.

'Is that where it hurts?'

She nodded. 'Yes,' she said, pulling away from him. Her skin seemed to burn where he'd touched it, and she wondered how that was possible.

'Don't worry about my falling down on the job,' she said quickly. 'I've taken some aspirin and . . .'

'What you need is a decongestant. There are some in the medicine locker.'

Nicole's eyebrows rose. 'Where do you find the time to practise medicine, Captain? Dramamine for queasy stomachs, decongestant for headache—I didn't know you were a licensed doctor.'

His lips drew away from his teeth in a cold smile. 'If you knew anything about the sea, if your boyfriend had taught you to read any of the instruments in this cabin . . .'

Her chin lifted. 'What does that have to do with practising medicine without a licence?'

'The barometer's been falling for the past few hours.'

Nicole laughed politely. 'I'm sure that's fascinating, Captain, but what does it have to do with my headache?'

'The drop in air pressure's affecting your sinuses, Nicole. It's a common reaction. Aspirin won't help, but a decongestant may.'

Nicole sighed. Yes, she thought, he was right. She'd had the same problem once in Chicago, when a storm had blown in over Lake Michigan. It was too bad she hadn't thought of it herself.

'All right,' she said with a grudging shrug of her shoulders. 'Thanks for the advice. I'll try it.'

'And when you've done that, make some coffee and bring me a cup.'

Her eyes met his. 'Aye aye, Captain.'

'And secure things down here.'

'Things *are* secure. I . . .'

Chase bent down and picked up the book she'd been reading. 'I said, secure things,' he snapped. He tossed the book to her and she caught it. 'Is that clear?'

'Perfectly clear,' she said tightly.

He looked at her and grinned. 'Maybe you could learn to add a salute to that,' he said softly. 'It would make for a nice finish.'

She ground her teeth together as she watched him go up the companionway, and then she threw the paperback the length of the cabin. It hit the panelling and fell to the floor in a flutter of torn pages.

'You'd like that, wouldn't you?' she muttered softly as she stalked to the medicine locker and wrenched it open. 'That would suit you just fine, Captain.' She peered at the array of neatly labelled phials, pulled one out, and tapped a tablet into her hand.

Damn the man, anyway, she thought as she swallowed it. At least he was dependable. You could always count on him to remind you of just what a rat he was.

She slammed the locker shut and looked into the mirror above the sink. She really did look like hell, she thought, running her fingers through her tousled hair. Her hazel eyes seemed enormous in her pale face. Well, at least her headache had accomplished something. She and Chase had said more to each other in the past minutes than in the day that had gone by since they'd seen the trawler yesterday.

Nicole stepped into the cabin and sighed as she began to pick up the scattered pages of Billy's book. All that fuss about the fishing-boat, and for what? In the end, it was obvious the trawler's crew hadn't even seen them. The boat had steamed past far astern, Chase said when he came below to set her free.

By then, it seemed as if hours had dragged by. Nicole's lips were dry from the press of his handkerchief, her wrists were chafed, and whatever insanity had possessed her when he'd kissed her, whatever she'd thought she'd felt when is mouth touched her, had long since fled.

There had been plenty of time to reach a cold understanding of what had happened. Her frazzled brain had taken panic and exhaustion, mixed them together and blended the result into something far less terrifying than the truth, which was that Chase Tarrant hated Aston enough to take whatever was his, whether it was a boat or a woman.

'The trawler's gone,' he'd said as he untied her ankles. 'I'm sorry about this, Nicole, but you gave me no choice.'

She muttered something around the wad of linen, watching as he unbound her wrists. When he finally untied the gag, she spat it out in a rage.

'Yes, sir,' she said. 'I understand, sir. Very good, sir. Is there anything else, sir?'

For a moment, her heart seemed to stop beating. Chase's eyes turned to ice as he stared at her. A muscle knotted in his jaw, his mouth narrowed until it was a thin line.

'You forget yourself, Nicole,' he whispered finally. His lips turned up in a smile that chilled her to the marrow, and his hand drifted lightly over her cheek, along her jaw and to her throat. 'Don't push your luck.'

Her eyes followed him as he rose and walked to the companionway ladder. He grasped the railing alongside the steps and turned back to her.

'Billy keeps his things in the forward locker.' His voice was expressionless. 'Fine yourself a change of clothing.'

'What I'm wearing is fine,' she said stiffly.

'I said, find yourself a change of clothing. We'll be sailing into warmer weather. If you collapse because of the heat, I might be tempted to cool you off overboard—*permanently*.'

Billy's locker turned out to be a treasure trove of softly faded jeans, denim cut-offs, and T-shirts. Nicole stripped off her grimy clothing, showered, and pulled on shorts and a shirt. The shorts fitted well, although the shirt was large.

Just as well, she thought, staring at herself in the small mirror over the sink. She had no bra. She hadn't worn one under her sweatshirt—she never did under something so loose—but then, she hadn't planned on a long sea-voyage, either. She'd thought they would have to turn back once she'd put the boat out of action.

Suddenly, she thought again of the feel of Chase's mouth on hers and the swift, velvet brush of his tongue. Her cheeks blazed with humiliation.

'Do you see what he's doing?' she whispered to her reflection. 'He's trying to dominate you any way he can. He . . .'

'Nicole! Get your tail on deck. Let's find out how little you know about sailing.'

She smiled ruefully at herself. There was a certain bitter satisfaction in having discovered his game plan.

She spent the balance of the afternoon listening to him

bark at her.

'A ten-year-old can steer a better course than that.'

'The mainsail's still luffing. Haul it in.'

'You call that stowing a sail?' He pulled the big spinnaker she'd so laboriously folded out of its bag and kicked it. 'Do it again.'

By the time she went below to make supper, she was exhausted. She'd brought Chase his meal, then ate her own and cleaned the galley. At sunset, she'd sat on the edge of her bunk and yawned.

If I could just close my eyes for a moment . . .

The next thing she'd known, it was morning. She had no idea where Chase had spent the night. On deck, probably, because the berth facing hers—his bunk—hadn't been disturbed as far as she could see.

Except that his blanket was missing. No, not missing, exactly. When she'd awakened, the blanket was draped over her. Nicole had clasped it to her, imagining how Chase must have stood beside her and watched her as she slept, how his hands must have brushed her body as he'd covered her . . .

'Nicole! Where the hell's that coffee?'

His harsh voice brought her back to the present. She pushed the hair back from her face and stuffed the torn paperback book into the bin.

'In a minute,' she called. 'I'll bring it right up.'

By the time the percolator was bubbling, *Enchantress* was rolling more heavily. Nicole half filled a mug with coffee, then made her way cautiously up the ladder. A gust of wind almost blew her off her feet as she stepped on deck. Chase caught her arm.

'Your coffee,' she said, raising her voice a little so it would carry over the sounds of wind and water. 'I didn't fill the mug—I thought I'd probably spill it because . . .'

'Where's your life-jacket and harness?'

'Below. I . . .'

He took the mug from her and turned her towards the cabin. 'Get them and put them on. Never come on deck without them.'

'But I'm not staying,' she said.

'Will you stop arguing? Get the damned things!'

She sighed. 'Yes, Captain,' she muttered under her breath as she climbed down the companionway ladder. Actually, staying topside for a while might not be a bad idea. The fresh breeze would probably blow away the lingering remnants of her headache.

When she came on deck again, Nicole was carrying her own mug of coffee. The boat rocked wildly as she stepped through the hatch. Chase grasped her arm, steadying her as he hooked her lifeline to a cleat, and then eased her to the seat beside him.

'How's your head feeling?'

'Much better,' she admitted. 'The decongestant did the trick. I'd never have remembered that low pressure could cause it.'

'Sometimes you can feel a change in weather before your instruments show it. You just have to learn to listen to what your body's trying to tell you.'

Nicole's eyebrows rose. 'Somehow,' she said drily, 'I can't imagine you with a sinus headache, Captain.'

Chase laughed and rubbed his left forearm automatically. 'How about an arm that's been broken twice? It's almost as accurate as the weather bureau.'

'Broken twice? In boating accidents?'

'Nothing so exciting. The first time I was working a cat at a construction site.'

'A what?'

'A cat. A caterpillar tractor—you've seen them, they're the big machines that move earth at construction sites. I hit a soft spot and it tipped, and I . . . well, I got off easy. I'm lucky it was only a broken arm.'

Yes, she thought, watching him surreptitiously, yes, she could just imagine him operating one of those giant machines, the sun beating down on his broad shoulders, the sweat beading on his muscled arms . . .

He turned towards her and she looked down at her coffee.

'And the second?' she asked.

He shrugged. 'A guy's boat slipped off the cradle while I was scraping the hull.' He grinned. 'My arm was the only part of me that didn't get out in time.'

'A guy's boat? Wasn't it yours?'

'Hell, no. I couldn't have afforded to buy a rowing-boat those days, much less a sailing-boat. I used to do odd jobs on the docks, trade my muscle for a day of sailing.'

Nicole smiled. 'Sort of a barter system, hmm? Did it always work?'

'Usually.' His mouth twisted. 'Of course, there was always someone who didn't want anything to do with riff-raff like me.' Suddenly, he got to his feet. 'We'd better get the boat ready, Nicole, I have the feeling we might be in for a rough night.'

She stood, grasping the rail for support as she followed his gaze. Stars blazed coldly overhead, and a full moon lay a milky path across the sea. Only the increasing wind and swelling waves hinted at any change.

'The sky's so clear,' she said. 'Are you certain?'

'The only thing I'm certain of is that there's a low-pressure centre that's been building ever since we passed the Contessa Islands.'

His voice was calm, but she sensed an underlying tension. A chill moved along her spine. 'Can't we go around it?'

She saw the quick flash of his teeth as he laughed. 'That's exactly what I've been trying to do. I've laid a new course twice in the past two hours, but the storm seems determined to come our way.'

Nicole laughed, too, and she wondered if the sound of her laughter seemed as artifical to Chase as it did to her.

'You say that as if it were alive.'

'It is. None of the forces of nature are static, Nicole, especially when you're at sea.'

'But all that equipment below, those computers and things . . .'

He nodded. 'They're the best there is. But all that stuff can do is present me with data. Meteorology is an art more than a science. It still comes down to taking your best guess.'

Nicole drew in her breath. 'Will it be . . . do you think it's going to be bad?'

It seemed forever before he answered. 'Perhaps.'

'Worse than the one the day we left Coral City?'

His voice was almost gentle. 'That wasn't a storm, Nicole. It was just a strong breeze and a touch of rain.'

A strong breeze and a touch of rain. A fist knotted deep in her belly as she remembered the heaving sea and the plunging boat. She took a breath.

'All right, Chase,' she said. The name came easily to her. 'What shall I do? You said we had to get the boat ready.'

Chase nodded. 'I'll take care of things up here. You go below. Make sure everything's secured. Then make some sandwiches. And more coffee.'

'Anything else?'

'Yes.' He touched her shoulder and she turned towards him. It was hard to see him clearly in the moonlit night, but she thought his lips curved in a quick smile. 'One last thing,' he said softly. 'Don't be afraid.'

'I'm not,' she said, too quickly. 'I . . .'

'Nicole.' His eyes met hers. 'We'll be fine. This is a strong boat—I had her designed to stand up to the roughest seas.' His fingers moved lightly over her cheek. 'Trust me,' he said. 'I'll take care of you.'

Below, in the cabin, she moved from locker to locker, making sure they were tightly shut, picking up the one or two things she'd missed before and putting them away. By the time she finished the sandwiches and filled the thermos, *Enchantress* was beginning to pitch up and down in the waves.

She thought of the little bronze plaque hanging in the cabin of Aston's boat. It was an old sailor's plea, something about asking God why he'd made the ocean so big and the boats that sailed it so small. The worst she'd ever faced on *Fortune's Fancy* was a light summer rain, but if she had to be on a boat, sailing into the teeth of a storm, she'd rather it be on Chase's boat with Chase at the helm.

Hold on! What was wrong with her? This wasn't Chase's boat, it was Aston's. Where was her loyalty, her conviction, her commitment to right and wrong . . .?

'How's it going?'

Chase was standing at the bottom of the companionway steps. 'Fine,' she said brightly. 'How are things on deck?'

He was soaked, she saw, his hair plastered to his head, the water dripping down his face. His shirt and jeans were dark with rain.

His brows drew together. 'The damned engine won't turn over.'

'The engine? I don't understand.'

'Neither do I. Powell may have skimped on the maintenance. But Essex should have checked things

over.' He saw the look on her face and he shrugged.
'Don't worry about it. I'd have preferred to have more
distance between us and the reefs around the Contessas,
but there's no sense complaining about what's done
when you can't right it.' He reached for his rain gear
and began pulling it on. 'I've doused the headsail and
double-reefed the main.'

She laughed shakily. 'I don't suppose you could try
that in English?'

He gave her a quick smile. 'It means we're going to
give the wind as little sail area as possible. We'll ride this
one out.'

A giant hand lifted *Enchantress,* held her suspended
in mid-air, then slammed her into a trough. Nicole
stumbled and Chase caught her by the shoulders.

'I'll help you on deck,' she said quickly.

'No!' His fingers cut into her flesh. 'You're to stay
below.'

She shook her head. 'No, I'm coming with you.
You'll need me.'

'I want you to stay here.'

Nicole drew in her breath. 'Chase . . .'

'Have a little faith, lady. I'm one hell of a terrific
sailor. Haven't I told you that?'

He smiled into her eyes. It took all the courage she
had, but finally she managed to smile at him in return.

'All right,' she said. 'I'll stay below. But if you need
help . . .'

'I'll let you know. I . . .'

A roaring filled the cabin, a noise of such power and
strength that it sounded as if a train were bearing down
on them. Nicole clutched at Chase's sleeve, staggering
against him as the boat shouldered through a wave and
then rolled sickeningly in its trough.

'What was that?'

Chase bent his head until his mouth was at her ear. 'It's the wind,' he yelled. 'The storm caught us, Nicole.'

Her heart rose to her throat as she looked at him. There was a smouldering fire behind the grey ice of his eyes. He looked, she thought suddenly, like a man about to set off on the advanture of his life.

'Chase . . .'

He grinned and drew her to him. 'Some day, you'll tell your grandchildren about this night.' His mouth covered hers in a breathtaking kiss, and then he was gone.

What she'd tell her grandchildren, she thought as the hours dragged by, was how slowly time passed when you wanted it to speed it along. But she'd never be able to describe the power of the storm as it tried to claim *Enchantress* for the sea.

The wind was a cacophony of banshee voices wailing a tune played on the devil's pipe-organ as it wailed through the shrouds. Nicole sat braced in her bunk while the boat pitched and rolled with drunken abandon.

She stared towards the companionway, all her thoughts riveted on Chase and what he must be facing alone on deck. What if he were in trouble? What if he needed her? Even if he called to her, she'd never hear him.

The cabin lights flickered, dimmed, flickered again, then went out. Nicole rose quickly, dredged a flashlight from the pocket of her slicker, and turned it on. She trained its beam on the companionway ladder, scrambled up the steps, and peered through the hatch window.

'Chase?'

Her shout was a whisper against the roar of the wind and the sea. If only she could see him, just for a moment. Was he all right? The power of the storm was all around them, the ocean slamming against their fragile craft with punishing force. Suppose he'd forgotten to hook up his lifelife. Suppose, even wearing it, he'd been swept overboard?

Her heart began to race. If only she hadn't taken Billy's place—Chase needed a crewman now, a *real* crewman. Why had she been so stupidly vindictive because of what he'd done to Aston?

Aston had nothing to do with it, Nicole, a voice suddenly said inside her head.

What he'd done to her, then. That was why she hated him . . .

Come on, come on, stop lying! You don't hate Chase, you never have. You hate yourself for wanting him. How can you want a man who is everything you despise?

Something crashed to the deck above. The boat groaned like a wounded animal and rolled on its side. Nicole screamed Chase's name, then clawed her way through the hatch.

A gust of wind slammed into her, knocking her down as she reached the steeply canted deck. She hung on for her life as she snapped her lifeline to a cleat and peered into the storm.

Spray and foam filled the air. In the half-light of the storm, the sky and sea seemed intermingled. Waves high as houses towered over the boat, then fell to smash down on the deck and run off into the sea.

She shouted Chase's name again, but the storm threw her cries back to her. Bent against the wind, Nicole started to crawl forward, but was stopped by a mass of tangled wire and cordage.

The mast was down and half over the side, its heavy weight heeling *Enchantress* at an insane angle. The hungry sea was already lapping across her deck. Between the broken mast and the storm, she would capsize and sink. And Chase was gone, he was . . .

'Nicole.'

'Chase,' she sobbed, and she crawled into his arms, crying and laughing at the same time. 'You're alive. Thank heaven! I thought . . .'

He bent to her, put his lips to her ear. 'We have to cut the mast free. If we don't, it will sink the boat.'

She nodded and fell to her knees, inching her way along the tilting deck, holding aside the tangle as he cut through the steel cables that still held the mast to the boat. At last it was free, and together they pushed it over the side.

Enchantress rose slowly from the terrible angle at which she'd been lying. Chase put his arm around Nicole and pulled her to her feet.

'. . . below,' he yelled.

It was the only word she understood. He dragged her to the companionway and she half fell into the cabin, with Chase following. She swayed back against the ladder as he secured the hatch.

'I heard a crash,' she gasped. 'I thought . . . I thought you . . .'

'The mast went down. I don't understand it.' He pushed back his hood and looked at her. 'Are you all right?'

She nodded. 'What do we do now?'

The boat heaved beneath them, and Chase caught her to him. 'We ride out the storm,' he said.

Nicole swallowed hard. 'Can we? I mean, will we . . .?'

'We're probably through the worst of it.' He peeled off his rain gear, then sank down on the edge of his bunk. 'Where's that thermos of coffee you made?'

She switched on a portable lantern and set it on the table. 'Candlelight,' she said with a shaky smile. 'Here's the coffee. And the sandwiches.'

Her hands trembled as she filled a cup and handed it to him. Then she took off her rain gear and sat down beside him, watching as he drank the coffee in quick gulps. His eyes were red-rimmed, his face gaunt with exhaustion. When he was done, he reached for a sandwich and bit into it as if he were famished.

'You'd better have something, too, Nicole. It may be a while before we get a chance at a meal.'

She nodded. 'Coffee. Not anything solid. I'm afraid I might . . . I might . . .' Her voice broke.

'Nicole?'

She turned her head away and waved her hand. 'I'm fine. Really. I . . .'

Chase sighed. 'You're damned right you are.' She looked at him in surprise and he smiled and put his arm around her. 'That was good work before, Crew. Very efficient stuff.'

She felt the sting of tears behind her lashes. 'Chase, I'm sorry . . .'

He made an impatient sound and drew her into the curve of his shoulder. 'Don't waste your energy talking,' he said in a gruff voice. 'Relax and try to get some rest.' She felt the quick brush of his lips against her temple. 'You've earned it.'

She sat silent for a moment, taking comfort from his closeness, and then she sighed.

'I feel so guilty,' she said. 'If I hadn't . . .'

She looked at him and her voice trailed away. Chase had fallen asleep, his arm still clamped securely around her. Nicole smiled, then sighed and closed her eyes. The storm still raged around them, but here, in this warm little world of their own, held close in Chase's arms, she was safe.

She awoke to a wrenching crash. Her eyes flew open in horror. The stern of the boat rose up, then fell back, and she and Chase were thrown to the cabin floor. Water was pouring into the cabin through a gash in the hull.

'Chase? What is it? What . . .'

He lifted her in his arms and pushed her to the ladder. 'Hurry,' he yelled. 'Go on, Nicole. Move!'

He grasped her waist, propelling her through the open hatch to the deck. The storm was raging; wind-driven water was everywhere, stinging her cheeks and eyes. Chase shoved past her, pulled the inflatable life-raft free of its housing and tossed it into the heaving sea where it snaked open.

'Jump, Nicole!'

Into that? Into that fragile toy bobbing in an angry sea? But Chase's hands were on her shoulders, his strength was her strength. Nicole took a deep breath and tumbled from the sinking boat into the rubber raft. Within seconds, Chase was beside her. He cast off the line that secured them to the boat, then gathered her into his arms.

'Hold on to me, love,' he said. 'I won't let anything happen to you.'

She wanted to tell him she believed him. But, as the life-raft lifted with gut-wrenching swiftness on the crest of a wave, she saw a jagged line of rocks rushing towards them. The raft was slammed against the reef and capsized, throwing its human cargo into the raging ocean.

As the sea rolled over her, Nicole's last thought was that it would be better to die with Chase Tarrant than to never have known him.

CHAPTER EIGHT

NICOLE lay sprawled on a white sand beach, caught in the shadowed world between sleep and reality. Her head hurt, although she couldn't imagine why. She'd taken the tablets, just as Chase had told her, and the pain had gone away.

She touched her forehead and winced in surprise. There was a lump just above her eyebrow—had she hit her head? Yes, she must have, she must have fallen down or something, because it wasn't just her head that hurt, it was everything. She ached all over. And her lips were dry—they tasted of salt.

Not salt. Salt water. An ocean of it, pouring into the boat, into the raft, swirling around her, around Chase . . .

She came awake with a terrifying suddenness, pulse racing and heart hammering. Sand grated against her palms as she pushed herself up and stared around her.

What strange world was this? Nicole raised a trembling hand and pushed her tangled hair back from her face. She was on a beach somewhere, a deserted half-moon of white sand that stretched down to placid blue water. Tall palm trees speared the blue-grey sky. She could hear the papery whisper of their dry fronds rubbing together in the warm breeze. But there was another sound, a deeper one, like the slow pulse-beat of a resting giant.

She winced as she lifted herself to her knees, paused, and then rose to her feet. The sand seemed to shift beneath her and she held her breath, waiting until the world steadied. She could see the source of the other sound now: across the calm water of the lagoon, waves pounded against a curving wall of rock, trying to gain access to the white sand at her feet. The ocean beyond the reef looked angry and dark and . . .

The reef.

Nicole's heart tripped erratically. Memory of the wreck returned with a vengeance that made her tremble. The reef had ripped the heart from *Enchantress,* torn apart the life-raft, and she and Chase had been cast into the sea.

Chase. Her breath caught in her throat. 'Chase,' she whispered. The wind caught his name and blew it away like an offering made to an uncaring god. Where was he? He was alive; he had to be. The sea couldn't have been so cruel; it couldn't have claimed Chase and let her live.

'Nicole.'

His voice tore the silence. She spun towards it in disbelief.

'Chase?' she whispered.

She stood frozen in time, half afraid the tall, broad-shouldered figure was the product of her imagination. Tears welled in her eyes, blurring her vision. She took a hesitant step towards him, and then another.

She flew across the sand to him, weeping with happiness. 'Chase,' she sobbed, 'I didn't know if . . . I was afraid you were . . .'

His arms closed around her and gathered her to him. 'It's all right,' he whispered. 'It's all right now, Nicole.'

Tears streaked the fine sand that powdered her cheeks as he held her and stroked away her fear. She closed her eyes and burrowed against him, breathing in the scent of his skin, luxuriating in the steady beat of his heart beneath her ear. Finally, he cupped her shoulders in his hands and held her from him while his eyes searched her face.

'I'm sorry you were alone when you awakened. I wanted to be with you so you wouldn't be frightened.'

She laughed shakily and wiped the back of her hand across her nose. 'I thought you . . . I thought something had happened to you.'

He shook his head. 'I'm fine.' He smiled and gently stroked her hair from her face. 'How do you feel now? The last time I asked, you said your head felt like an army was marching through it.'

Nicole looked at him in surprise. 'When? I don't remember.'

'About an hour ago. I wanted to make sure you were all right.' He touched the skin beside the bruise on her temple and she drew in her breath. 'Does that hurt?'

'A little.'

'Yeah, I'll bet it does. You've got quite a bump above your eyebrow.' He stepped back and ran his eyes over her slowly from head to toe. 'Does anything else hurt?'

She gave a little laugh and shook her head. 'No, not really. I mean, I feel as if I've been run over by a truck, but nothing's broken or anything.'

He smiled and put his arm around her waist. 'Come on, let's walk. You'll feel better if you get your muscles moving before they stiffen up.'

Nicole looked up at him as they began walking slowly towards the water. 'What happened to us, Chase? How did we get here? And where are we? I . . .'

'How much do you remember?'

Her brows drew together. 'Not much,' she said finally. 'I remember getting into the raft. And then I remember it tipping over and the water closing over me.'

A tremor ran through her and he drew her closer against him. 'That's behind us now,' he said gently. 'We're safe.'

'Yes, but—but how did we get here? The reef . . .'

'We were extremely lucky. The wave that should have bashed us into that reef swept us over it and into the lagoon instead.'

She sighed. 'It's all a blank. I don't even remember banging my head.'

'You did that when you were thrown from the raft. I grabbed you and held on to you.' He shrugged his shoulders. 'There isn't much more to tell. The lagoon was bad, but I managed to get us to the beach.'

They reached the shoreline and stopped. The water lapped gently at their feet in stark contrast to the distant waves pounding against the reef. Nicole shuddered as she looked out to sea.

'I'd have died out there if you hadn't saved me,' she whispered. 'How long was I out?'

'You came to while I was carrying you across the sand. You said your head hurt, and I told you to close your eyes and just hold on to me.'

. . . His arms were around her. Her mouth was against his skin . . .

'You put your arms around my neck and sighed; when we reached the trees, I started to put you down, but . . .'

. . . but she clung to him as he lowered her to the sand and begged him not to let go of her . . .

Nicole's cheeks flushed. 'I don't remember anything,' she said.

Chase's arm tightened around her. 'Do you remember telling me you wanted to stay in my arms? You said you . . .'

. . . only felt safe there. Yes, yes . . .

'No,' she said quickly, 'no, I told you, there's nothing until I woke up a little while ago.'

He smiled into her eyes. 'The clouds looked as if they were building again. These weather systems double back

sometimes; I thought I'd better scout things out while I
still had the chance.'

'Do you know where we are? I mean, I know we're on
an island, but . . .'

Chase nodded. 'I'm sure this is one of the Contessas.'
He lifted her hair from her shoulders and let it fall across
his fingers.

'How do you know that?'

'There's no other landfall in this part of the Atlantic.'
His eyes darkened. 'I just wish to hell I'd been able to
start the engine. We might have been able to clear them if
we'd had power after we lost the mast.'

Nicole's eyes sought his. 'Chase? I . . . I'm really very
sorry about *Enchantress*.'

He gave her a quick smile. 'Thanks.'

'I know what she meant to you.'

He shrugged. 'I've never lost a boat before. It's a hell
of a feeling—I keep thinking there must have been
something I could have done to prevent it.'

'But you did everything you could. You mustn't blame
yourself.'

'It's not a question of blame, Nicole. It's a question of
responsibility.'

'You said yourself that Billy should have checked the
engine. And . . . and Aston, too. He . . .'

Chase smiled at her. 'That's very loyal of you, Crew,'
he said softly. 'But I was her captain. The responsibility
is mine.' He shook his head. 'It just doesn't make sense.
A brand new engine shouldn't refuse to start. And the
mast—hell, I've ridden out storms as bad as this one.
There's no reason that mast should have gone.'

He fell silent. His face was like a mirror, Nicole
thought as she watched him. His pain and guilt at the loss
of the boat were visible in the lines etched beside his
mouth, in the furrows between his dark brows. She

wanted to reach out and stroke the lines away, to put her arms around him and kiss his mouth until it curved with pleasure.

Her hands trembled and she jammed them into her pockets before they could betray her. What did she really feel for Chase Tarrant? Too many things had happened too quickly. She'd hated him, then admitted a grudging respect, and all the time there'd been something else, something that moved within her like wildfire when he touched her. It had frightened and confused her on the boat, and now here they were, alone, on a speck of land in the middle of an endless sea . . .

'Nicole?'

She blinked her eyes. 'Yes. I'm sorry, Chase. Did you say something? I was just—I was just thinking about . . . about . . .'

He clasped her shoulders. 'It wasn't important. I can try to figure out what went wrong later.' His grasp tightened. 'What *is* important is now, and getting through the next few days as best we can.'

Nicole laughed shakily. 'Yes,' she said, 'that's—that's exactly what I was thinking.'

'This island's not very big, but it'll provide us with the necessities. There are bound to be fish in the lagoon— and I found a stand of coconut palms, which means we'll at least have something to eat and drink until we take a better look around tomorrow.'

'If there are palm trees, doesn't that mean there's fresh water, too?'

Chase smiled. 'Give the lady a hand,' he said. 'I'd bet there's a spring somewhere.' He kneaded her shoulders gently. 'We'll manage, Nicole.'

'Chase? Will they—will they find us? I mean, we didn't send out a mayday call or anything.'

'Of course they'll find us. The "satnav" has been

sending back automatic position reports all along. That means our silence will be almost as effective as a mayday signal. The committee will notify the coastguard and they'll mount an air and sea search and concentrate it in the area where they last heard from us. After that, it's only a matter of time.'

A matter of time.

'How long, do you think?'

He shrugged his shoulders. 'Tomorrow, if we're lucky. Otherwise, three days—a week, at most.'

A week. A week alone with him.

He put his hand beneath her chin and tilted her face up to his. 'Don't look like that,' he said softly. 'The days of shipwreck victims living out their lives on deserted islands are long gone. It just doesn't happen any more.'

She managed a shaky smile. 'I hope you remember more about Robinson Crusoe than I do,' she said.

Chase grinned. 'Actually, all I remember is that he had Friday to do most of the tough jobs.' He slipped his arm around her shoulders and they began walking up the beach towards the palm trees. 'Opening our tea-time coconut, for instance.'

Half a dozen large fruits lay beneath a tall palm tree. The storm had apparently shaken them loose. A good thing, too, Nicole thought, as she looked up at the top of the tree. The thought of shinning up into the swaying crown was less than comforting. Chase bent and picked one up, hefting it in his hand while a thoughtful expression stretched across his face.

'It's probably half husk. But there's got to be a way . . .'

'My father always opens them with a hatchet,' Nicole said, and then she laughed. 'I guess that's not too helpful, is it?'

Chase sighed. 'Nope. But I've got an idea. Grab

another of those babies and let's take them down to the water. There,' he called over his shoulder as she followed after him, 'see? Where those rocks jut up out of the sand.'

A few jagged rocks gleamed wetly along the shoreline. When they reached them, Chase pursed his lips and stared at the coconut he held in his hands, turning it over and over carefully. Finally, he took a deep breath.

'OK. Here goes nothing.' Nicole flinched as he smashed the hard-husked fruit against the sharp edge of a rock. A piece of the husk flew off and landed in the lagoon. He lifted the coconut high over his head and brought it down on the rock again, grunting with the effort, and a long crack appeared in the husk. 'Gotcha,' he said, flashing a triumphant grin.

Nicole squatted down beside him. 'Is there anything I can do?'

He laughed. 'Yeah. Cross your fingers and hope for the best.'

She watched as he dug in his pocket and pulled out a clasp-knife. It looked old, the handle worn, the brass fittings shiny with age. But when he opened it the blade gleamed.

'The Tarrant Toolkit,' he said. 'A little long in the tooth, but it's never failed me yet. Let's see how it does on dinner.'

He dug the blade into the crack in the coconut's husk, forced it as deep as possible, and began to strip the dark husk away. Beads of sweat glistened on his forehead as he worked. Nicole's eyes moved across his shoulders. His shirt was torn in places from their battle with the sea; she could see the play of muscle beneath his skin as he wielded the knife. Flecks of sand clung to the fine hair on his arms and legs; there was some caught in his dark hair, too, dusting it with white.

She touched her tongue to her lips. They were less than a hand-span apart. All she had to do was reach out and touch him, brush the sand from his skin. She could almost feel the warmth of his flesh beneath her palm. And then Chase would raise his head. He'd look up at her, his grey eyes darkening with predatory anticipation as they had before, and then . . . and then . . .

He looked up. 'Ready?'

Nicole blinked. 'Ready?'

He gestured to the pieces of husk that lay at their feet. 'Here I am, about to perform a miracle, and the lady's not watching.' Chase smiled at her. 'Step two, coming up.'

She watched as he worked an awl-like blade into the core. A smile spread slowly across his face.

'Here we go,' he said, and he pulled the knife free and held the coconut out to her.

Pale, milky liquid trickled down its side. Nicole laughed, took the coconut from him, and raised it to her mouth. The milk was sweet and cool on her tongue—she thought that she'd never tasted anything more wonderful.

'Delicious.' She smiled and wiped the back of her hand across her lips. 'Here, try it.'

They passed the fruit back and forth until the last of the liquid was drained. Then Chase slammed the kernel hard against the rock until finally it cracked open, revealing its white interior.

'The main course,' he said with a quick smile. 'And now for a bottle of *vin ordinaire.*' He pierced the second coconut and then they carried their meal up the beach to the trees. The rich meat was sweet and filling, as was the milk. When they'd finished eating, Chase leaned back on his elbows and sighed with contentment.

'Good?'

'Better than good. That was probably the best meal I ever had.'

He rolled over on his stomach and smiled at her. 'We'll have to send our compliments to the chef.'

Nicole laughed and picked up his pocket-knife. 'Actually, we should send our compliments to this little thing,' she said, turning the knife over in her hands.

It was, indeed, old and worn, a sober country cousin to Aston's shiny red pocket-knife with its bristling array of gadgets. The knife in her hands looked like the kind of thing a boy might own.

'This looks as if it has a long history.' She looked at him and smiled. 'A boyhood souvenir?'

Was it her imagination, or did his eyes seem to grow shadowed? He reached out and took the knife from her.

'Something like that.' Chase closed the blade and ran his thumb along the worn handle. 'It's been with me a long time.'

'Well, it certainly came in handy today.'

He smiled crookedly. 'Yes,' he said softly. 'You might almost say it redeemed itself.'

Nicole's eyebrows rose. 'What's that supposed to mean?'

'Nothing, I guess.' He tossed the knife up, caught it in mid-air, then rose and stuck it into his pocket. 'OK, Miss Wheeler, it's time to check into the Contessa Hilton.'

'The Contessa Hilton, hmm?' She smiled as she got to her feet. 'Sounds good to me. Have the bellman bring our bags.'

Chase took her hand and they began to walk along the beach. 'Well, the management seems to have rented my usual suite. But, offhand, I'd say that spot just ahead would be adequate. What do you think?'

He pointed to where the land rose in a gentle slope to a stand of tall palms.

Nicole smiled. 'I always wanted an ocean view.'

'Sensible choice, Miss Wheeler.'

Suddenly, Chase stopped and turned to her. He cupped her face in his hands and she looked up at him. Their eyes met, and something sharp as an arrow, yet sweet as the memory of his kiss, pierced her breast.

'Nicole,' he said softly, 'in a few days, you'll be safe and and sound in Coral City. All this will just be a memory.'

Were his words meant as reassurance, or were they something more? Nicole forced a smile to her lips.

'Yes,' she said, 'yes, I know.'

Chase gave her a long, searching look. For a moment, she thought he was going to speak again. Instead, he put his arm around her shoulders and drew her close against him as they began walking towards the stand of palms.

'It's been a long day,' he said. 'Let's get some rest.'

Behind them, the white sand stretched in untouched beauty to the blue water of the lagoon.

CHAPTER NINE

NICOLE took a silvery fish from the palm leaf in which it was wrapped, placed it on a flat rock, and pulled Chase's knife from her back pocket. Sunlight reflected along the blade as she opened it. Then, tongue pressed lightly between her teeth, she bent over the fish and made a quick cut the length of its belly.

Even here, beneath the palm trees, the sun beat down with merciless power. Her cotton T-shirt was pasted to her skin; sweat dripped from her forehead and into her eyes. A swim would be wonderful, she thought longingly. And she'd have one, just as soon as she finished with these fish—assuming, of course, that Chase had left the lagoon by then.

She raised her head and looked towards the water. He was still there, a distant figure standing in the shallows, the sun glinting on his naked shoulders and back. Her glance fell lower. He'd stripped off his denim cut-offs and was wearing only dark-coloured briefs, just as he had late yesterday afternoon. Nicole swallowed drily and looked down at the fish lying before her. No, she thought, she certainly wasn't going in swimming while Chase was still in the lagoon. She'd made that error once, and once had been more than enough.

It had happened yesterday. They'd eaten more of the coconut meat, then fallen asleep, sprawled in the sand beneath the palms. When they awoke, the sun was beginning to slide towards the horizon.

'Wouldn't it be nice if the Contessa Hilton had hot

showers?' Nicole had asked with a wistful smile.

'How about a hot bath?' Chase had asked. 'Will that do?'

In a second, they were both racing down the beach to the lagoon, laughing as they splashed into its warm water. Nicole had been so grateful to wash away the sand and sweat that coated her that she'd thought of nothing else—until, still laughing, they'd run back to the beach.

'That was wonderful,' she said, turning to Chase. 'I feel so much bet . . .'

Her words trailed away as their eyes met. His smile fled, and his face darkened with desire. She wanted to look away from him, but she couldn't. Water glinted in the dark hair that curled on his chest; drops of it beaded on his muscled shoulders. His eyes moved over her slowly, and suddenly she realised that her wet T-shirt was clinging to her breasts, that her nipples had tightened under his gaze and were thrusting against the fabric.

'Nicole,' he whispered.

A slow wave of heat curled through her body. The shock of her own need ricocheted through her, frightening her with its intensity, and she turned away, fearing yet hoping he'd come to her. But the moment slipped away, and they both dealt with it by pretending it had never happened.

It had, though, and there was no forgetting. During the next hours, they had treated each other with polite reserve, as if the storm hadn't swept them past the constraints of their old relationship. Dinner, of more coconut and coconut milk, was eaten in silence, punctuated only by impersonal comments about the improving weather and the beauty of the setting sun.

As night fell, they settled in the sand, several feet

apart. A crescent moon rose in the sky, casting its pale
light on them. Wind sighed through the palms, making
the fronds cast dancing shadows on the sand. Suddenly,
there was a rustling noise behind them. Nicole's nerves
reached breaking point and she sat up in a rush, heart
pounding, and stared into the inky shadows.

'What was that?' she whispered.

'Rats, probably,' Chase said in a matter-of-fact voice.

'Ah,' she said, trying for the same tone but not
achieving it, 'rats. Of course.'

Chase looked at her. In the moonlight, she saw the
quick curve of a smile move across his face.

'Let's sleep down the beach a bit,' he said, still in that
same casual tone, as if moving out from the trees were
something he'd simply decided to do.

When he rose and held his hand out to her, Nicole took
it gratefully, just as she settled down beside him in the
sand a few yards from the palms. She tensed when she
felt his arm curl around her.

'Come here,' he said gruffly, and before she could
protest he drew her close beside him. 'Relax,' he
whispered, his breath stirring her hair.

Never, she thought, listening to the beat of his heart,
feeling the rapid leap of her own. But after a while his
breathing grew deep and even, and she felt the tension
begin to drain from her tight muscles.

I'll just rest a while, she thought, closing her eyes.

It was the last thing she remembered until the morning
sun awakened her and she opened her eyes to find herself
alone. She scrambled to her feet, searching the beach
with mounting anxiety, telling herself it was foolish, after
all. Where could he have gone to? And yet, when at last
she saw him, waving to her as he trotted towards her
through the sand, her heart leaped with joy.

'Breakfast,' he said with a boyish grin, and he held out

a large, brightly coloured fish.

'You caught that?' she asked foolishly, and he laughed.

'Yup. Scout training pays off, after all. I made a weir out of palm leaves and branches—a trap,' he said when she looked puzzled. 'And it worked!' He slapped the fish down on a flat rock, sat down in the sand, and pulled his knife from his pocket. 'How do you feel about *sushi?*'

Nicole sighed. 'Not good,' she said, squatting beside him. 'Fruit and vegetables are all right raw, but fish is supposed to be cooked.' She smiled. 'But somehow I have the feeling I'm going to learn to love it.' She watched Chase for a moment and then clucked her tongue impatiently. 'Here, give me that knife. You're supposed to lift out the backbone with one stroke.'

Chase looked at her. 'Are you telling me you know how to clean a fish?'

She smiled archly as she took the knife from him and swept the blade neatly and cleanly the length of the fish's bony spine.

'I spent my childhood years learning the art from a pro. My father,' she added, when Chase's eyebrows rose. 'He was—*is*—the best fisherman I ever knew.'

Chase grinned and rose to his feet. 'In that case, I'll leave you to it while I put up a pot of coffee for breakfast.' He lifted a coconut from the sand and hefted it from one hand to the other while he watched her fillet the fish and lay the pieces on a palm leaf. I've never eaten *sushi* that colour,' he said doubtfully. 'But what the hell, how bad can it be?'

The question turned out to be a rhetorical one. The fish was edible, if you swallowed each mouthful with enough coconut milk, but the flesh was oily and the taste strong. Still, it was food, rich in protein, and they both forced down all they could manage, until at last Nicole groaned and pushed the remaining scraps away.

'Another mouthful and I'll . . .'

Chase nodded. 'My sentiments exactly. Let's bury the rest so the rats don't think they've been invited to a feast, and then we'll explore the island.' He rose and held out his hand. 'Water's the next priority item. We can probably manage with coconut and the liquids from whatever fish we trap, but I'll feel a lot better if we can find fresh water somewhere.'

It had taken less than an hour to explore their tiny universe. The island was small and crescent-shaped. The inner curve of the crescent, the one protected by the reef, was a paradise of white sand and palm trees. The outer curve was far wilder. The ocean beat ceaselessly at the shoreline, and shells littered the sand. A low outcropping of rock rose inland, and it was there they found the spring.

Nicole wouldn't have recognised it as that. She saw only a trickle of water oozing from a rocky cairn. It was Chase who yelled, 'Water!' as if he'd found the gold of El Dorado.

'Where?' she asked, and he laughed and grasped her by the waist.

'Right at our feet,' he said, lifting her off the ground so that she was laughing down at him. He whirled her around in a dizzying dance. 'Water, water everywhere, and now there's some to drink!'

Nicole had put her hands on his shoulders and smiled. 'With due apologies to Coleridge,' she'd said, 'I think you've improved his poem, Captain Tarrant.'

He'd grinned. 'Do you really, Miss Wheeler?'

And suddenly the laughter was gone. His eyes had turned dark, the pupils widening until Nicole felt she might fall into them. Chase had whispered her name while he lowered her slowly, the hard length of his body like a caress against hers.

'Nicole,' he'd said again, his voice thick as they'd stood looking into each other's eyes, his hands splayed on her hips so that she felt the demanding pressure of each finger against her flesh, their bodies so close that she knew how urgent his need for her was.

Even now, hours later, she could still remember the intensity of those moments. Anything might have happened, she thought, closing her eyes, but a cloud had passed over the sun, blocking its heat and light with shadow, and they'd both looked up. It had been enough to cool the tension that had mounted between them and they'd separated.

'You're liable to cut yourself if you hold the knife that way.'

She looked up, startled, as Chase's voice brought her back to the present. He stood beside her, hands on his hips.

'I . . . I didn't hear you coming,' Nicole said quickly. 'I guess I was daydreaming.'

He smiled. 'Didn't your father teach you not to let your mind wander while you're using a knife?' He sat down cross-legged in the sand beside her, peered at the fish she'd already cleaned, and whistled appreciatively. 'He sure as hell taught you everything else.'

'I told you, Daddy's the . . .' Her voice trailed into silence. Chase was so close that she could smell the clean, salted scent of the sea on his skin. He'd put on his cut-off denims again. The sun had faded the threadbare shorts almost white and darkened his tanned skin to a honeyed bronze.

'. . . the best fisherman in the world. So you said.' He smiled and brushed an errant strand of hair from her cheek. 'Where did this world-class fisherman teach you to fillet fish?'

Nicole smiled. 'Lots of places. I grew up in a little town about thirty miles from Chicago, a place called Dayton. Daddy sold men's haberdashery all week, but he lived for vacation trips to Sturgeon Bay.'

Chase smiled. 'Another Chicago suburb?'

She laughed. 'Sturgeon Bay? No, not at all. Sturgeon Bay's in Wisconsin. It's Daddy's idea of paradise.'

Chase leaned back on his elbows. 'Were you a willing pupil? Somehow, I just can't picture a little girl putting down her dolls and picking up a fish knife, no matter how much she loved her daddy.'

'I never thought about it. Learning to clean his catch was as natural as breathing. He always took me fishing with him, from the time I was little.' She looked up and grinned. 'I can bait a mean hook, too, and I can cast a fly right in your eye.'

Chase rolled on his side, dug his elbow into the sand, and propped his head on his hand. 'And what did your mother have to say about all this?'

Nicole smiled. 'She thought it was fine. It meant she didn't have to face cleaning fish herself any more.'

He grinned. 'She isn't a fishing nut, hmm?'

'Mama?' Nicole laughed softly. 'Hardly. Piano's her passion. She's a good teacher—she taught me to play whenever Daddy wasn't teaching me to fish.'

Chase smiled. 'Didn't they ever argue about whether it was time to fish or go to a concert?'

'Mama's a great believer in talking through a problem. "How about next weekend at Lake Winnebago?" Daddy would say, and Mama would say that was fine, and wouldn't he love to go to the symphony tomorrow night? They always worked it out.'

A strand of dark hair fell over her eyes again. Before she could toss it back, Chase reached out and stroked it away from her cheek.

'It sounds like a good life.'

Nicole nodded. 'Yes, it was.'

His hand lingered on her cheek. 'But not good enough to keep you there. Why did you leave? Did you want to see the world?' He laughed softly. 'Or are those Illinois winters as bad as I've heard?'

She drew in her breath. 'It was . . . it wasn't anything like that. I . . .' She hesitated and then looked at him. 'I got married.' Her words were clipped. 'And then I got divorced. When it was over, I decided I needed a change of scenery.' She looked at Chase and then away. 'I married the wrong man for the wrong reasons.'

Her admission surprised her. She knew it was the truth—she'd known it for a long time, even before her marriage had ended—but she'd never admitted it to anyone else before, perhaps because it seemed such a raw admission of failure. Why, she wondered, had she been so ready to admit the truth to this man she barely knew?

Chase sat up. 'What happened?' he asked softly.

Nicole shrugged her shoulders. 'I was barely nineteen. Tony lived in Chicago. He was in Dayton on business . . .'

'A sophisticated man from a sophisticated city. And he swept you off your feet.'

She blinked. 'How did you . . .' She blew out her breath. 'I guess it's not an unusual story, is it? Yes, that's what happened. Dayton's a small town. Population five thousand on a good day, that kind of thing. Everybody knows everybody—I don't know if you can picture what that's like.'

His smile faded. 'Yeah,' he said softly, 'yeah, I sure as hell can. Church suppers, high school dances, the Boy Scouts . . .'

Nicole looked at him in surprise. 'Yes. Exactly. The boys I'd grown up with were like . . . They were boys.'

She fell silent. It had been a long time since she'd allowed herself to remember how Tony had arrived in Dayton, scouting locations for a new plant, longer still since she'd let herself dwell on how impressionable she'd been. To Nicole at nineteen, Tony was the answer to a young girl's dreams.

Chase's voice drew her back. 'Does it hurt you to talk about it?'

Nicole shook her head. 'No, not the way you mean. It was a long time ago. It's just—I guess it always hurts to remember something painful.'

A muscle tensed in his jaw. 'Yes. It does.'

'You sound as if you know all about small towns. Did you grow up in one, too?'

'Me?' His smile was quick and, she thought, forced. 'I grew up in a town that makes Dayton sound like a big city.'

Nicole laughed softly. 'Impossible.'

Chase leaned over and took the knife from the sand where it lay. 'Kingsport, Virginia.' Again, that quick smile flickered across his face, like a lamp lit against the dark and then snuffed out. 'Main Street, with *the* traffic light, a hardware store, two bars, and a grocery. That was it.'

'And you couldn't wait to get away?'

His eyes met hers. She thought, for a moment, she saw a dark anger glowing in their grey depths.

'That's right,' he said finally. 'I'd been living for that moment as long as I could remember. Even when I was just a kid . . .'

His words drifted into silence. After a moment, Nicole touched his arm.

'Come on, it can't have been that bad. I mean, being a kid in a town like that is OK. You know everybody, you have got lots of friends . . .'

Chase flipped open the knife and ran his thumb along the worn blade. 'Was there a poor family in Dayton? You know the kind I mean—every whistle-stop has one special charity case, the family that gets free turkeys and hams at Christmas and Easter, the one where the kids always dress in everybody else's hand-me-downs.'

Nicole nodded. 'The Halversons. They were such nice people, but Mr Halverson had some kind of illness and Mrs Hal . . .' She looked at him. 'Is that how . . . was your family . . .?'

'Poor?' He laughed and flipped the knife into the sand. The blade sank deep into the white grains. 'Yes. And nobody ever let us forget it. Not the minister who prayed over us, not the ladies' auxiliary that hand-delivered the food baskets, not my fifth-grade teacher who asked the kids in my class to bring in warm clothing for me one winter when . . .' He drew in his breath. 'Hell, until I was ten years old, I thought my name was "That-Poor-Tarrant-Kid".'

Nicole touched his arm again. His muscles felt like coiled steel beneath her palm.

'Maybe you misunderstood them,' she said gently. 'Maybe you saw it from a child's perspective. Surely people meant well? They wouldn't . . .'

'What kind of town was Dayton? I mean, what kind of people live there?'

'All kinds, I suppose. I don't understand what you mean.'

He shrugged free of her hand. 'Rich people? Middle-class people? It's not a very complicated question.'

The harshness in his voice surprised her. 'Middle-class people, I guess. But I still don't . . .'

Chase laughed hollowly. 'Everybody's got money in Kingsport. Old money. It's one of those towns built around the whims of the wealthy. It's less than an hour

from Washington, DC—it was a summer resort at first;
now it's a suburb for those who can afford it. Heaven
alone knows what the Tarrants were doing there. They've
always been poor—fishermen, some of them, or
labourers. That's what my father was. He broke his back
wielding a pickaxe and a shovel so the rich pigs could
have swimming pools and gardens and . . .'

Suddenly, she thought she understood everything. 'Is
that why . . .' Nicole drew in her breath. 'Is that why you
hate Aston? Because he's—because he's . . .

'Because he's rich?' He laughed softly. 'Hell, if I hated
people who had money, I'd have to hate myself. I've
done all right since I waved goodbye to Kingsport.'

'Then . . . then why . . .?'

His eyes burned into hers. 'I told you why,' he said
coldly. 'It's because of the way Powell does things. He's
so damn typical—the rich stick with the rich. They play
together, they work together, they use their money to buy
people . . .'

'I know you're talking about Aston, Chase, about the
things you say he's done . . .'

Her words ran together and she fell silent. Suddenly, it
was vital to set everything straight, to prove once and for
all that Aston wasn't guilty of using his money and
influence to buy people. If she could do that, then Chase
would stop believing that Aston's money had bought her,
too.

'Listen,' she said quickly, 'if Aston had done anything
wrong, I'd know it.' Her eyes met his. 'I'm his secretary,
Chase. Maybe—maybe your opinion of him is just a
carryover from your childhood. Maybe you're still bitter
about receiving charity and . . .'

He lunged forward and yanked the pocket-knife from
the sand. 'Do you see this knife?' he demanded in an
angry whisper. 'Yesterday, you said it looked as if it had

been with me a long time.' He snapped the blade closed
with his thumb and held the knife in his outstretched
hand. 'Well, you were right. I've had this since I was
eleven. That's when I won a contest run by the Kingsport
Scout Troop 223.'

She stared at him, wondering at the change that had
come over him. the easy smiles of the past day and
morning were gone, replaced by a bitterness she
remembered all too well from their first encounters.

'Chase, what does this have to do with . . .?'

She gasped as his free hand closed around her wrist, his
fingers pressing on the fragile bones.

'The troop put the knife on display in a case in the
school lobby. It was so beautiful! The handle's walnut
with ebony inlay—you can't tell it now, but back then it
was so polished you could almost see your face in it. The
deal was that the scout who got the greatest number of
new merit badges that year would win the knife. The
scoutmaster promised they'd have your name engraved
on a little plaque and it would be mounted on the
handle.'

Nicole's eyes fell to the handle; there was no plaque,
only the faint outline of Chase's initials that had long-ago
been scratched into the wood. His gaze followed hers and
he nodded.

'Yes, that's right. My name's not on it.' He leaned
towards her. 'The son of the town's high and mighty, a
kid who hadn't got anywhere near the number of badges
I had, was the winner.' A cold smile twisted across his
face. 'I went to the scoutmaster. I said, "Hey, this isn't
right, I won. You know I did." And he said, "Yeah,
Tarrant, you did. But old man Gimbel had his heart set
on his son coming in first, and the Gimbels are pretty
high-powered people. I wish I could do something, but I
can't. The Gimbels endow the troop, kid, they bought

that uniform you're wearing . . ." '

'Chase,' Nicole said softly, 'listen to me . . .'

'I told him I wouldn't stand for it. I told him I'd tell the whole town the truth—and he laughed. He said nobody would believe me, that they *wanted* the other kid to win, didn't I understand that? He said if the knife meant so much to me he'd buy me one out of his own pocket . . .'

He got up abruptly and stared out to sea. Nicole rose and took a step towards him, her heart breaking for the boy whose hopes had been dashed that long ago day, certain now that she held the key to understanding the man Chase Tarrant had become.

'No wonder you kept the knife all these years, Chase. I understand.'

He turned towards her so quickly that she shrank back instinctively. 'No, you don't,' he said in a voice she didn't recognise. 'You don't understand at all.'

'I do. You were treated unfairly and it still hurts to remember.'

His hands shot out and clasped her shoulders. 'How much does Powell really mean to you?' he demanded.

The unexpected question took her by surprise. 'Aston?'

'Yes,' he growled, 'that's right.' She winced as his grasp on her tightened and he shook her roughly. 'Tell me, dammit. I want to know.'

'Aston is—he's a good friend,' she said. 'He's my boss . . .'

'And he wants you.'

There was a curious flatness in his voice and in his eyes. 'Yes,' she said slowly, 'he does. He . . .'

She cried out as he pulled her into his arms and kissed her. His mouth was rough on hers, his embrace so hard that she felt as if her ribs were about to break. A wave of alarm vibrated through her, and she put her hands flat on his chest and tried to push him away.

'Chase,' she said, 'listen to me. Don't . . .'

His eyes were fierce. 'Don't?' He twisted the word as he echoed it, warping it with evil. 'Is that what you tell Powell when he takes you in his arms?' His arms tightened around her. 'Do you play the same game you've been playing with me the past few days?' He thrust his hands into her hair and pulled her head back until she was staring up into his face. 'Playing with a man, turning him on and off as if he were a light switch, is dangerous stuff, Nicole.'

'That's not what I . . .' Her voice trembled, then broke. 'Chase, please, you're frightening me. I haven't played with you. I . . .'

His lips drew back from his teeth. 'Maybe Powell likes playing games. But I don't. I never learned how—I was too busy surviving.' His fingers tangled in her hair and he cupped her head while his thumbs traced rough arcs along her cheekbones. 'I'm still waiting for an answer, Nicole. What do you say when Powell takes you in his arms?' His eyes narrowed until they were slits. 'Answer me, damn you!'

The metallic taste of fear was on her tongue. How could things have changed so quickly? Chase was changing before her eyes, he was turning back into the man she'd at first thought him to be.

'Stop it,' she said.

'Has he bought you, the same way he's bought everything else?'

'How can you ask such a thing?'

She gasped as his arms curved around her waist and he pulled her against him. 'Do you think I forget the reason you were on my boat?'

'I didn't know you then,' she said. 'Please . . .'

His voice was ice. 'What makes you think you know me now?' His body moved against hers, hard and heated with power. 'Did you think I'd change into a pussycat because I told you a story about a poor, dumb kid?' His eyes grew black as midnight. 'The dumb kid got smarter, Nicole. He learned that the only way you get what you want is to take it.'

'You bastard,' she whispered. 'You almost had me thinking you . . .'

His lips twisted. 'Tell me now. Do you belong to Powell?'

Her hesitation was as brief as the blazing path left by a shooting star. 'Yes,' she hissed, 'that's right, I belong to Aston.' Her chin lifted and her eyes, shining with tears, met his. 'And I never play games with him, I never stop him from making love to me, I . . .'

She cried out as Chase bent her back over his arm and covered her mouth with his. His kiss was hard, filled with the rage that had turned him back into the man she'd always known he was. It stole her breath away, it terrified her—and yet . . .

A slow lick of flame sprang to life deep in her belly, spreading its heat in a steady upward blaze that rose through her until it reached her breasts. Chase's mouth moved on hers, his lips urging hers to part, his tongue demanding entry. She felt his hand slide up her back, beneath her shirt, felt the heat of his fingers as they spread along her flesh.

His mouth left hers; she felt the warmth of his breath on her neck, then the sharp nip of his teeth on her skin.

'I should have done this the first time I saw you,' he said in a rough whisper. His hand moved across her skin and she groaned as he cupped her naked breast. 'You wanted me then, just as I wanted you.'

'No. That's not . . .'

His mouth took hers again with an urgency that set her blood pounding. When he lifted his head, she was breathless.

'And that night at the club . . .' She cried out as he swung her into his arms. 'I should have taken you away from all those phonies and their games and lies, and carried you to *Enchantress* and thrown you on the bunk in the cabin.'

Her heart was going to leap through her ribs, she thought wildly. It was racing crazily, out of control with fear—fear and something else, something deep within herself that was even more terrifying than the darkness in Chase's eyes. Nicole twisted in his arms and beat her fists against his chest.

'Put me down. Damn you, Chase Tarrant . . .'

He laughed down at her. 'You can stop pretending, Nicole. I'm only going to do what we've both wanted all along.' He caught her wrists in one hand as he strode rapidly along the beach. 'We might as well make the best of our island paradise.'

Tears welled in her eyes as he lowered her to the sand and lay down beside her, one leg thrown over hers, pinning her beneath his weight.

'Look at me.' His voice was harsh and urgent. Nicole raised her lashes slowly and stared into his face. 'Tell me you want me.'

'Never. Never, Chase. I don't . . .' She caught her breath as his hand moved over her, stroking her body from breast to thigh.

'Tell me, Nicole.'

She shook her head wildly. 'No. I don't. I . . . Oh, please, let me . . .'

'Say it.' His mouth brushed hers; she felt the rasp of his tongue on her lips and a shock went through her. 'Say it,' he whispered. His body trembled against hers, and suddenly his voice grew soft. 'Nicole, lovely Nicole.'

She looked up at him. His eyes were still dark, but something in them had changed. The terrible anger had fled; there was a vulnerability in his face that stunned her. He whispered her name again and stroked her cheek, and then bent to her and kissed her.

His mouth moved against hers with a sweet gentleness. He said her name again, the sound a sigh against her lips, then drew her into his arms, holding her against him, his hand moving over her with tender urgency. Slowly, Nicole felt her body begin the response to his that she had so long resisted.

He made a sound in the back of his throat that was a growl of triumph. 'Yes,' he whispered, 'yes, love, that's right, open to me.'

'Chase.' Her eyes closed and she breathed his name as his lips moved along her throat. 'Chase . . .'

'Nicole.' She looked up at him. 'I want you more than I've ever wanted any woman, more than I've ever wanted anything.' He bent his head and brushed his lips over hers. 'Tell me you want me, too, Nicole. Say it.'

Her answer was in her eyes. She lifted her arms to him, hesitantly at first, and then she curled them around his neck and drew him down to her, down into the heat and the longing they'd both denied. He kissed her until she was dizzy with the honeyed taste of his mouth, until her lips were swollen with pleasure, and then he sat her up and slowly eased her shirt over her head.

She watched him through half-lowered lashes as he saw her naked body for the first time. She felt herself bloom beneath his hot eyes, felt her nipples tighten and bud, felt her thighs grow slack with desire.

'You're so beautiful,' he said, the words whispering over her skin, his lips and tongue moving like silk on her throat and breasts. His mouth closed around her nipple and she cried out, her body arching towards his. 'So beautiful,' he whispered as he stripped away her cut-offs. 'My Nicole.'

His hands moved over her, learning the curve of hip and belly, the juncture of thigh and groin. She moaned when his fingers caught beneath the lace band of her panties; she lifted her hips from the sand, crying his name breathlessly as he slid them from her, and when his hand cupped the essence of her that was woman, she sobbed aloud with pleasure.

'Chase,' she said, running her hands along his shoulders, free at last to explore the warmth of his skin and the power of his muscled shoulders. She touched his chest, burying her fingers in the dark whorl of hair.

He caught his breath. 'Yes,' he said fiercely, 'yes, love.'

She watched as he stood and drew off his denim shorts. It was he who was beautiful, she thought, so proudly and powerfully male. When he came to her again, she took him in her arms and held him to her, thrilling in the rapid beat of his heart against hers and the satiny feel of heated flesh on heated flesh.

'Tell me what you want,' he whispered. 'This?' He kissed her hard, his tongue silken against hers. 'This?' He drew her nipple into his mouth and she cried out, the cry rising to a long, breathless sigh as his fingers found her, stroked and entered her. 'Tell me,' he said again, 'Nicole . . .'

'You,' she sobbed, 'I want you. Chase, please, please, I want . . . I want . . .'

She cried out as he entered her, sobbed his name as he plunged into her with a passion that matched her own. He moved slowly at first, then more quickly, and she wrapped her arms around him, curled her legs around him, her body alive with response to his.

'Chase . . .'

Her voice broke and he kissed her. She heard him whisper something against her throat, and she thought it might be her name; she hoped it might be a promise; she prayed it was his assurance that he understood what she felt, that he welcomed it, that he shared it with her . . .

I love you, Chase.

The realisation came with such clarity that it stunned her. Why had it taken her so long to recognise the truth? She loved him; she'd loved him all along; she would always love him.

'Chase,' she said urgently, 'I . . .'

But it was too late to tell him. 'Nicole,' he groaned, 'my love.'

She caught her breath, cried out in wonder, then soared with him into a new world of incredible beauty in which love and desire were one.

CHAPTER TEN

CHASE was driving a huge caterpillar tractor across a sea of sand towards Aston, who sat smugly behind a desk littered with dollar bills and pocket-knives . . .

The sound of the tractor's engines changes, turned from a roar into a whine—the whine of a plane.

Nicole's eyes flew open and she awoke, heart racing as she looked into the sky. A plane! There was a plane dipping low over the water, coming straight towards the island.

She started to sit up, but Chase murmured in his sleep and his arm curved more closely around her. She looked down at him and touched his cheek.

'Chase,' she said urgently, 'Chase, wake up!'

His eyes opened slowly and focused on her face. 'Hello, love,' he said softly. A smile curved across his mouth. 'How long have you . . .?' His smile froze, then vanished, and a look of shocked excitement took its place. 'Listen,' he whispered. 'A plane!'

He rolled away from her. Before she could move, he was struggling into his shorts, getting to his feet and racing down the beach.

'Hey,' he yelled, waving his hands wildly over his head, 'hey, you up there—here we are!'

Nicole held her breath, watching as the plane dropped out of the sky. The roar of its engines filled her ears as it flashed overhead and waggled its wings from side to side. Chase spun towards her and raised his fist into the air.

'He saw us!' The smile on his mouth split the dark

146

stubble along his jaw and cheeks. 'He saw us, Nicole! Do you hear me? He saw us!'

She sat up, blinking in the glare of the late-afternoon sun. For some reason she couldn't understand, she felt as if she were still asleep, as if she were moving with the slowness of a dream-figure while she pulled on her T-shirt and shorts and then rose from the sand.

They'd been found. But—where was the exhilaration? She felt nothing but a disquieting kind of numbness as she watched the plane angle back out over the water, then fade into the distance.

Chase turned towards her, still smiling. 'I said they'd find us in just a couple of days, didn't I?'

Surely it had been longer than that? It had been a lifetime . . .

She nodded. 'Yes, that's what you said.'

He grinned happily and clasped her shoulders. 'A couple of hours from now, we'll be drinking rum and Cokes in Charlotte Amalie. How does that sound?'

'Great,' she said quickly. 'It sounds great.'

Dammit, what was the matter with her? In just a little while, they'd say goodbye to this little island forever. No more rats scurrying through the palms, no more terrible-tasting raw fish, no more blazing sun and sandpaper winds and . . .

'Nicole,' Chase said, 'Nicole, listen.' There was an urgency in his voice. 'We have only a little time before they come . . .'

She looked into his face and suddenly she was afraid. He was right; they had only a little time, and there was so much to say. That was why she felt this curious sense of disappointment: she understood it now. Their rescue had come too soon—there hadn't been time to tell each other all the things that mattered.

But they would take care of that now. Chase would tell

her that he knew she'd never belonged to Aston, just as she would tell him that she knew that what Aston had told her about him had been wrong. During the long afternoon, only their bodies had spoken of love, but now they would give voice to what they felt, they would unravel the dark skein of misunderstanding that had brought them together . . .

The whomping beat of helicopter blades filled the air with sound that drowned everything else as a chopper dropped slowly from the sky and settled on the tight-packed sand beside the lagoon.

Chase's arm slid to her waist and Nicole looked up at him. She thought his lips formed her name, but whatever else he said was lost in the sound of the spinning rotor. But it was all right: there would be all the time in the world to talk when they reached safety.

She was stunned at the size of the crowd waiting for them in the Virgin Islands' port of Charlotte Amalie. Apparently, the loss of *Enchantress* and the subsequent air-sea search had drawn heavy media coverage. They stepped from the helicopter and were trapped in a sea of microphones and a glare of flashbulbs, until representatives from a local yacht club freed them and took them in tow.

Nicole watched helplessly as a florid-faced man herded Chase towards one car and a matronly woman in a frilly summer dress drew her into another.

'Please,' she said, 'I want to . . .'

'Of course, dear,' the woman said in a soothing voice. 'You want a hot bath and a meal and a change of clothing. We've made all the arrangements at the club.' She smiled as the car sped along a road that curved beside the sapphire ocean. 'We're so happy you're all right, dear.' Her eyes sparkled. 'Your Mr Powell will be especially delighted.'

Nicole looked at her. 'Aston? Is he here?'

'Since the start of the search, Miss Wheeler. He's told us all about you—that you were so disappointed at his decision to sell his boat to Mr Tarrant that you stowed away on it yourself.' The woman patted Nicole's arm. 'They're trying to reach him—he's out in a chartered plane, looking for you.'

Aston. She didn't want to see him. Not yet. When she told him she'd fallen in love with Chase, he'd be hurt. And she hated hurting him. Chase and Aston had made all kinds of accusations about each other, but she suspected the truth was simply that they didn't understand each other. They probably never could.

She leaned her head back. What she needed, she thought as the car sped silently along the curving road, was some time to get herself together. A long soak in a warm bath, then a nap, and then she'd face Aston. Yes, that was how she'd do it.

The clubhouse was a sprawling white structure built on a rocky promontory above the sea. Nicole paused as she stepped from the car and looked back down the road. Her escort took her arm.

'Come, my dear. Let me show you inside.'

Nicole drew back. 'I was hoping to see Mr Tarrant.'

The woman smiled. 'Of course. He'll be along soon, I'm sure.'

Nicole nodded, then let herself be led into the cool, dim interior of the building. The desk clerk beamed at her.

'Welcome, Miss Wheeler. We're delighted to see you.' His smile broadened. 'Mr Powell's radioed a message. He says to tell you he's very happy you've been found and that he'll be here as soon as possible.'

She nodded wearily. 'Thank you. I wonder—I'd like to

leave him a note.'

The man handed her a pen and paper and she hesitated, fighting against the sudden urge to take the coward's way out with a note instead of facing Aston and telling him to his face that she'd fallen in love with Chase.

But her sense of decency prevailed. She scrawled a few hasty lines, telling Aston she was well and asking him to give her time to bathe and rest before seeing her. Then she signed her name, folded the note, and slipped it into an envelope.

'Please see that Mr Powell gets this the moment he arrives,' she said, handing the sealed envelope to the clerk. 'It's important that . . .'

'Nicole.'

She looked up, startled with pleasure at the sound of Chase's voice, but before she could speak her self-appointed guardian moved between them.

'Come, my dear. Your room and bath's all ready, and the kitchen's sent up a pot of hot tea. Doesn't that sound nice?'

Nicole looked at Chase and gave him a helpless smile. He'd been surrounded by club members, all eager to ask him questions about the storm that had sunk *Enchantress*. She sighed and gave up the uneven struggle.

'Yes,' she said, letting her benefactress lead her up a broad stairway, 'it sounds wonderful.'

The warm, scented bath was a luxury she'd dreamed of during the past days. When finally she stepped from the tub and wrapped herself in an enormous towel, her tensions had drained away. She smiled as she caught a glimpse of herself in a floor-to-ceiling mirror. How different she looked, she thought. The sun had put golden streaks into her chestnut hair and tanned her to the colour of pale toast.

But there was more to it than that. There was a softness around her mouth, a glow to her skin. Love had done that, she thought, and her heart filled with joy. Chase had done it.

She snapped on a soft lamp beside the turned-down bed, shrugged off the towel, and climbed beneath the light blanket. She yawned, then yawned again. An hour's nap, she thought drowsily, and then she'd face Aston. And then . . .

There was a knock at the door to her suite. Nicole sat up quickly and tossed the covers aside. Chase, she thought with a rush of pleasure. He'd shaken his watchdogs and come looking for her.

There was a robe at the foot of the bed and she pulled it on, barely noticing the fragile beauty of the thin blue silk. The knock came again, impatiently this time, and she tied the sash of the robe quickly and raced into the sitting-room.

'Yes, all right,' she called, 'I'm coming, Chase, I . . .' But when she flung the door open, her smile fled. Aston Powell stood before her.

Nicole drew in her breath. 'Aston,' she said slowly. 'How . . . how nice.'

His eyebrows rose. 'How nice, Nicki? Is that the best you can manage?' He smiled as he stepped into the room and closed the door behind him. 'I was hoping for a better greeting than that.'

His eyes swept over her, and Nicole was suddenly aware of the way the silk robe clung to her damp body. She flushed and crossed her arms over her breasts.

'I'm very happy to see you, Aston. It's just that . . . didn't you get my note?'

He laughed. 'You've turned into quite the little letter-writer, Nicki. First that cryptic note you left in my office and now this silly thing telling me to wait—as if I could.' His eyes narrowed and he took a quick step forward.

'Darling Nicki,' he said, pulling her into his arms, 'how I've missed you.'

Nicole put her hands against his chest. 'Aston, listen to me . . .'

His arms tightened around her. 'To think you did all this for me.'

'Aston, please, you don't underst . . .'

His mouth closed hungrily over hers. She stood rigid for a moment, hoping his kiss would be swift, but his lips parted and he drew her closer to him, until their bodies were pressed together.

The feel of him quickening against her made her shudder and she twisted her face away from his.

'Don't,' she gasped. But he ignored her protest; his body rubbed against hers, his mouth sought hers, and finally she slammed the heels of her hands into his chest as hard as she could. 'Let go of me, Aston.'

He drew back and stared at her. Silence stretched between them, and finally his hands dropped to his sides.

'That's all right, Nicki. I know you must be worn to a frazzle.' His eyes swept over her again, lingering on the outline of her breasts beneath the thin robe. 'You look . . . fine.'

Nicole drew in her breath. 'I *am* fine,' she said. 'I . . .'

But he wasn't listening. He was staring at her body, the expression on his face unsettling. She touched her tongue to her lips and swallowed hard.

'Look, why don't I get dressed? I'll only be a minute.'

'Nicki.' His voice was harsh; she winced as his hand closed on her arm. 'Nicki—what happened?'

Their eyes met. His questions were visible and desperate. Nicole swallowed again.

'I explained all that in the note I left in your office,' she said, deliberately pretending she'd misunderstood what he'd asked. 'I was angry, and I thought if I could find a way to stop Chase from winning . . .'

'Chase.' His voice was flat. 'Is that how it is now, Nicki?'

She took a deep breath. 'If you'd just let me put some clothes on . . .'

His hand tightened on her. 'I want the truth, Nicki, the truth about Tarrant and you.'

Nicole's eyes met his. 'You were wrong about him,' she said softly.

A knot of muscle moved in his cheek. 'Wrong? About Tarrant?' A cold smile flashed across his face. 'Hell, no, I wasn't wrong about him. He's everything I said he was.'

She shook her head. 'He's not. He's good and decent and . . .'

'He's a liar. A cheat. I told you all about him, Nicki. He's bribed his way into jobs he couldn't get on the up and up. He's cut corners and bought people. He . . .' His eyes narrowed. 'I'm disappointed in you, Nicki. Why would you believe any nonsense he may have told you? The man's completely without honour.'

Her head lifted sharply. 'He told me something about the race two years ago, Aston. He said you had a new sail flown out. He spoke to the sailmaker and to the pilot.'

What had she expected? Denial, certainly. Anger, of course. But not this—not the sudden flush that spread across Aston's cheeks, not the quick tightening of his lips.

'That's water under the bridge,' he said stiffly. 'Besides, who would believe him? The club members have known me for years, Nicki; they knew my father and my father's father.'

The rich stick with the rich.

'And he told me about *Enchantress,*' she said, watching his face. 'He said he'd commissioned her; he said . . .'

'I really don't want to discuss this, Nicki. All right, it might be difficult to prove who'd commissioned the design; that's why I decided not to fight him. I . . .'

'You said it had to do with the new municipal contract. You said . . .'

His breath hissed. 'What is this, Nicki? Are you going to take his side against me, after all we've been to each other?'

Nicole shook her head. 'We've been friends,' she said quietly. 'Nothing more.'

'I asked you to marry me, Nicki. I offered you my name.'

'And I'll always be grateful for your proposal. But . . .'

'But?' An awful smile curled across his mouth. 'Don't tell me, darling.' His voice grew soft and ugly. 'A week alone with Chase Tarrant has changed your mind.'

Nicole drew in her breath. 'Aston, please, don't make this any harder than it is. Chase and I . . .'

' "Chase and I".' The words became obscene. 'Ah, Nicki, Nicki, I love the way you say that. When did it become "Chase and I"? During the long ocean voyage, hmm?' His mouth was a livid slash in his white face. 'Those berths are cosy, aren't they? Barely big enough for two.' His eyes measured her coldly. 'I seem to have misjudged you, Nicki. I should have figured a woman like you . . .'

What was he talking about? Nicole stared at Aston Powell as if she'd never really seen him before.

'A woman like me?' she said slowly.

'I was a fool to let the pretty package blind me. Your type could no more have fitted into my world than Tarrant could.' Aston thrust out his bottom lip. 'Who the hell did he think he was, coming into Coral City as if he belonged here? My family's been here for generations.'

Nicole closed her eyes. 'You really did all the things Chase accused you of, didn't you?' she asked softly.

'That son of a bitch, thinking he could do whatever . . .'

'Aston.' Her voice was flat. 'I'd like you to leave now.'

Aston took a shuddering breath. When he spoke again, his voice was under careful control.

'Nicki, forgive me. I . . . I don't know what came over me.'

'It doesn't matter,' she said coldly. 'I just want you to go.'

He shook his head. 'Please, Nicki, I didn't mean any of it. I was upset. Look, I've sent for some champagne—it should be here in a minute.'

She looked at him as if he were crazy. 'Champagne? After the things you just said? Aston, please . . .'

'Nicki.' A tremulous smile tilted the corners of his mouth and he took a quick step forward and caught hold of her shoulders. 'Don't let it end like this. We've been friends for too long to finish on such a bad note. Can't you find it in your heart to forgive me?'

Nicole drew in her breath. Aston smiled, the charming, boyish smile she knew so well.

'Come on, darling. Tarrant's won your heart, I know that. But you can spare me this one evening, can't you?' His eyes pleaded with her. 'We'll open the champagne, raise a glass to old memories, and then I'll take you out to dinner. There's a little inn up the road . . .'

She shook her head. 'You're not listening, Aston. It's all over. I'm sorry, but . . .'

'I understand that,' he said quickly. 'But—but surely, for old times' sake . . .'

'I can't. Chase will . . .'

'Chase.' The word hissed from his mouth, but before she could say anything, the smile was on his face again. 'All right, how's this? I'll call Tarrant's room and tell him to meet us for dinner. Look, I know what you're thinking, Nicki, that he hates me and I hate him, but we're both grown men.' He spread his hands in a gesture that was at once imploring and innocent. 'He's won, and I've lost. At least let me show you I'm a gracious loser.'

Nicole hesitated. 'I don't think . . .'

Aston clasped her shoulders gently and turned her towards the bedroom. 'I *do* think. So why don't you get dressed—there's something pretty in the bedroom closet —and comb your hair, and I'll call Tarrant?'

'Aston, I still don't . . .'

'For me, Nicki. Please.' He patted her back. 'Go on,' he said softly, easing her into the bedroom.

The door closed behind her. Nicole leaned against it for a moment and then she sighed and moved towards the rumpled bed. Why had she let Aston talk her into this? she thought, opening the robe and slipping it from her shoulders. She could hardly imagine Chase agreeing to talk with Aston, let alone sitting at the same table.

She heard a murmur of voices in the sitting-room. The champagne Aston had ordered, she thought, and she rose and walked slowly to the cupboard. There was a dress hanging inside, just as Aston had promised, even a stack of silk and lace underthings on the shelf. She took them out and looked at them blindly, then tossed them on the bed.

The murmur of voices seemed louder, and a quick smile came and went on her face. Knowing Aston, he was probably complaining about the kind of champagne that had been sent. Not that it would matter to her or to Chase . . .

Lord, what was wrong with her? Even if, by some

miracle, Chase agreed to have dinner with Aston, how could she arbitrate their mutual hatred? It was an impossible situation, a disaster just waiting to happen.

Maybe it wasn't too late. If Aston hadn't called Chase's suite yet, if she got to him in time . . .

Nicole turned to the bed, reached for the underthings she'd tossed there, then shook her head impatiently. Getting dressed would waste time, and there was none to be wasted. Even now, Aston might be picking up the telephone. She snatched up the silk robe, pulled it on, and tied it around her waist.

'Aston,' she said, wrenching open the bedroom door, 'listen, don't call Chase. There's no reason . . .'

Her words tapered into silence. She stared into the sitting-room in disbelief. Aston was lounging against the wall, a smile curved across his face. His jacket was off, his tie gone, his shirt unbuttoned to the waist.

'It's too late, darling,' he said lazily. 'Tarrant's already here.'

Her eyes flew to Chase, Chase wearing a painted on smile, Chase with a look of such cold hatred in his eyes that she felt the chill of it stab through her heart.

'Chase,' she said, moving towards him, 'I . . . I didn't know you were here. I . . .'

The cold, terrible smile twisted. 'Yes,' he said, 'so I see.'

His eyes moved over her, taking in the curves of her body so visible beneath the clinging robe. Nicole felt her heart stop beating, then begin again like a runaway train.

'No,' she said, 'you don't understand.'

His eyes moved beyond her, to the open bedroom door where the rumpled bed stood centred in the softly lit room, and he smiled.

'It's *you* who doesn't understand, love,' he said softly. 'Powell and I were just comparing notes. After all, we have so much in common. First *Enchantress*, and then you. Of course, they're not exactly the same.' His eyes glittered dangerously. 'I mean, getting the boat was so much more difficult.'

The ugly words fell on her like a blow. 'Don't,' she whispered.

His eyes were grey pools of darkness. 'I've known what you were from the beginning,' he said softly. 'Only a fool wouldn't have known, and only a saint would have turned you away.' He smiled. 'And I've never been either.'

This couldn't be real, she thought desperately. This wasn't the Chase Tarrant she loved, this was the Chase Tarrant Aston had described, a cruel, selfish man who needed to win at any cost.

A moan rose in her throat. 'No,' she murmured, 'no.'

Chase's hand closed around hers. 'I have a gift for you,' he said, his voice filled with malice. 'A little souvenir of our island sojourn.'

She looked down as he drew her fingers open and pressed his battered pocket-knife against her palm.

'I don't—I don't . . .' Her voice broke and tears filled her eyes. She blinked them back and raised her eyes to his. 'I don't understand.'

His smile was swift and cold. 'Do you remember what I told you about this knife?'

'I . . . I don't see what . . .'

He closed her fingers tightly over the knife. 'Do you remember?'

Nicole nodded. 'Yes. You . . . you said that the scoutmaster bought it for you to make up for what had happened . . .'

Again, that wolfish smile spread over his face. 'No,' he said, his voice so low she had to strain to hear it, 'no, that's what he wanted to do. But that wouldn't have been good enough.' His hand pressed down on hers and she winced. 'I waited until they'd given the knife to the Gimbel kid, and then I beat him up and stole it from him.' His teeth flashed in quick grin. 'Do you understand? I took his nice, shiny knife and I made it mine. I carved my initials in it so that even if he ever managed to get it back, he'd never forget that I'd taken it, that I *could* take it . . .'

'No!'

His eyes blazed. 'Yes,' he growled. 'There's always a way to win, Nicole, and I'll always find it.'

A sob tore from her throat. She pulled her hand free of Chase's and stumbled towards the bedroom. There was silence behind her, then the sound of a door closing.

'Nicki,' Aston said, 'Nicki, he's gone. Nicki, please . . .'

She slammed the bedroom door and leaned against it, trembling. Aston's voice pleaded with her to come out. Then, finally, there was the sound of footsteps and she heard the sitting-room door open and close again.

Slowly, her back against the door, Nicole sank to the carpet. She was still sitting there when the first hint of dawn appeared in the tropic sky.

CHAPTER ELEVEN

A COLD, vicious wind whipped across Sturgeon Bay and snapped at the wooden dock that jutted out over the grey water. Nicole shivered, turned up her collar, then jammed her hands into the deep pockets of her quilted jacket. It was spring, she thought, or so the calendar said. But winter still clung to the bay and to the land surrounding it.

She drew a deep breath, then let it out slowly as she stared across the water. Had it always been so barren here? Surely not—she'd loved it when she was a child. But her visits had been in summer, she reminded herself, when the land was green with life and the water sparkled beneath the sun. She'd never been here while winter held the bay in its icy grasp, reluctant even at this late date to give up to the encroachment of spring.

A boat moved slowly far out in the bay, its hull a dark smudge against the grey sky. Soon the bay would be crowded with pleasure-craft, fishing-boats, sailing-boats and powerboats, while their owners made the most of Wisconsin's all too brief summer.

Nicole sighed as she turned her back to the water. She'd be gone from here before then. Four months of imposing on her parents was long enough—not that either of them would ever admit that was what she was doing.

'We love having you here, Nicole,' they said whenever she tried to thank them for having taken her in.

But the little grey-shingled house the three of them

shared was cramped. It was a perfect retirement cottage—her parents had bought it just after her father had retired, along with the small bait and tackle shop that stood next door.

'I don't think I ever want to see another shirt or tie again,' her father had announced firmly.

Nicole smiled to herself. Well, he wouldn't see too many of them, not in this little town. He was happy—it showed in his smile. Her mother was, too, despite her amiable complaints about fish being tone-deaf and fishermen worse. And the little shop was thriving, ever since they'd added a simple take-away menu to its services. Things were quiet now, of course, but during the summer the shop was busy from dawn until dark.

'Who'd have dreamed it?' Nicole's mother had whispered the night before, as the two women washed the dinner dishes. 'I thought I'd end up thanking my lucky stars that we had our pensions and social security to support your father's little hobby.'

Her father had come into the tiny kitchen just then and frowned at the two of them.

'No talking behind my back, girls,' he'd said with fake bluster, and then he'd kissed his wife's cheek. 'Hurry up in here, woman, so you can come sit with the old man and keep him company.'

Nicole sighed as she reached the old wooden bench on the side of the bait shop. She sank down on it and leaned her head back, letting the weak spring sun coax a little warmth into her bones.

It was lovely that her parents were so happy together, even after all these years of marriage. It was just that sometimes—sometimes, their very happiness made her sorrow all the more bitter.

She'd look at them as they sat together at the dining-room table after dinner, playing cards or Scrabble, smiling at each other, laughing at some private joke, and suddenly she'd think of Chase, of how they'd worked together and laughed together and loved together . . .

'Nicole? Where are you rushing off to, dear?' her mother would say when she rose from her chair.

Nicole would mumble something about being tired and hurry off to the little guest-room in the eaves, where she'd spend the night tossing and turning in the narrow bed that had been hers in childhood, trying not to listen to the hushed voices from below, knowing that her parents were huddled together, whispering about her, trying to figure out why their only daughter had come stumbling home months before.

She hadn't told them very much, only that she'd decided Florida wasn't the place for her. As far as that went, it was true. Living in Coral City would have presented her with daily reminders of Chase Tarrant. As for her job with the Powell Corporation—that was over. She never wanted to set eyes on Aston Powell again.

But Aston had had different ideas. He'd been waiting for her as she shut the door of her suite behind her the morning after the rescue.

'Get out of my way,' she said coldly.

'I'm willing to forgive you your indescretion with Tarrant,' he said quickly. 'I suppose I can understand how it was. The man forced his attentions on you. I know his sort.'

For an instant, her eyes flashed fire. 'Yes, so you said last night. *My* sort, too, Aston. Remember?'

He caught her arm as she tried to brush past him. 'I was upset, Nicki. Surely you can understand . . .'

Her anger drained away in a sudden rush of fatigue. 'It doesn't matter,' she said, shrugging his words aside. 'I'll stay at my job until you find someone to replace me. And then . . .'

Aston's hand encircled her wrist. 'You can't leave me, Nicole. I won't permit it. I . . .'

She looked into his face, seeing for the first time the calculating selfishness in his eyes.

'*You* won't permit it, Aston?'

His mouth thinned. 'You heard me. How will it look to other people? They know Tarrant took my boat, they know he sailed with you on it—if you leave me now, they'll think he's won.'

Nicole laughed unpleasantly. 'I don't really care what "they" think, Aston. And I certainly don't give a damn which of you won.'

His face grew dark. '*I* care,' he said venomously. 'Don't you understand? That bastard's taken enough from me as it is. He had no right . . .'

She shook her head in disgust. 'I heard all this last night, Aston. You and Chase Tarrant can go on playing your little games with each other, but I'm not interested any more.'

'Nicki, I . . .'

'You're no better than he is—you lied to me from the beginning. You bribed and cheated . . .'

'Not about us, Nicki. Not . . .'

Angrily, she pulled her hand free of his. 'There never was any "us", Aston. You only wanted me because I was the first thing in your life that didn't have a price-tag on it. And last night . . .' Her voice caught, then broke. 'You used me. You made it look as if you and I had been in bed together.'

Aston drew a rasping breath. 'What else could I do? Tarrant held all the cards. You have to understand. I . . .'

'Believe me, Aston, I *do* understand. The truth is, you hate Chase Tarrant more than you ever cared for me.' Nicole drew in her breath. 'I just wish I'd never met either one of you. I wish . . .'

She cried out as Aston grasped her shoulders. 'You know what I wish?' The sound of his breathing was loud in the silent corridor. 'I wish to hell *Enchantress* had gone down with Tarrant on board. I wish I'd done more than cut the shrouds and ruined the engine batteries. I wish I'd . . .'

He broke off in mid-sentence and a look of horror spread across his face. Nicole stared at him without speaking, and then she shrugged free of his clasping hands.

'Goodbye, Aston,' she said coldly.

'Nicki.' He swallowed; she could see the muscles in his neck move stiffly up and down. 'Nicki, listen, I didn't mean that. It isn't true. I . . . I just got carried away . . .'

'You don't have to worry; I won't tell anyone.' A terrible smile crossed her face. 'After all, I tried to sabotage *Enchantress,* too, in my own way.'

She started past him, her footsteps echoing along the polished parquet floor. After a moment, he called after her. 'You can't do this to me!'

Nicole turned and looked straight at him. 'I wouldn't try and enter any more races, though,' she said softly. 'There's no telling what kind of gossip might reach the rules committee if you did.'

She had no idea how either man got back to Florida. Ther was a flight just leaving the airport when she got there, and one seat left on it. Her seatmate was an elderly woman who tried to strike up a conversation even before the plane left the runway. Nicole smiled politely, then turned to the window and stared blindly out.

She was packed and on the road long before she'd given any thought to where she was going. 'No forwarding address,' she told her landlord. It was only after she'd passed the Georgia border that she realised there'd be nowhere to send her final pay-cheque. She shrugged the thought aside. She had enough money in her current account to get by for a while, if she was careful. If she went home . . .

The very thought made her feel better. She smiled for the first time in what seemed like forever. At first, it seemed strange to think of Sturgeon Bay as 'home', but by nightfall of that first day Nicole knew that trading the warmth of the Florida sun for the chill of a Wisconsin winter was the best idea she'd ever had.

It took two days to drive a distance that should have taken three or more. She drove tirelessly, the miles and the hours speeding by, stopping only when the needle on the fuel gauge neared 'empty' or she felt the need of a cup of hot coffee. When her old car began making strange, sputtering noises she ignored them, pushing both the car and herself past endurance.

And all the while she thought of nothing. Her mind seemed blank—no, she thought, as night fell in Tennessee or Missouri or wherever she was, no, her mind wasn't blank. It was a sponge, soaking up whatever nonsense the car radio fed into it. News reports, weather forecasts, singing commercials for bread and coffee and toilet-tissue were all tumbled together in her head like leftovers floating in a thick soup.

Every now and then something surfaced, some unbidden memory of herself in Chase's arms, and Nicole would pull to the side of the road and sit, trembling, until the ugly images were gone. Then she'd shift the car into gear and pull into the traffic again.

She telephoned her parents from Green Bay. 'It's me,' she said with a forced laugh. 'You'll never guess where I am, Mama.'

To her immense relief, they'd heard nothing of the

wreck of *Enchantress*—it was only after Nicole had been on the road that she'd wondered if news of the shipwreck and search might have travelled this far. She'd known it was doubtful—the race wasn't an event of importance in the Great Lakes area. Besides, the papers would have used her married name—Wheeler—not her maiden one, because, although she'd reverted to being addressed as 'Miss', she'd always kept the name Wheeler—it had seemed too much trouble to change it.

But, after a day or two of evading questions about why she'd left her job and her new life in Florida, she decided to tell them something of what had happened.

'I decided I deserved a change of scene,' she said, and she managed a little laugh. 'You see, I've had enough of tropical beaches in the past week to last me forever.'

Her parents paled as they listened to the story, even though she made it sound light and funny.

'You stowed away on someone's boat?' her mother said. 'But who was he?'

Nicole shrugged her shoulders. 'Just a business acquaintance of Aston Powell's,' she said. 'No one special.'

Her father put his arm around her. 'I'd like to meet this guy. He saved my little girl's life.'

'No,' she said quickly, 'no, he didn't. We . . . we were practically on top of the Contessa Islands when the boat sank.' She looked away from the two worried faces. 'Tell me about this place,' she said briskly. 'How's business, Daddy?'

Something in Nicole's voice made her mother shoot her father a warning look. They slipped smoothly to another topic, but Nicole knew Mae Sorensen sensed there was more to the story and her daughter's sudden appearance than met the eye.

'Do you want to talk about it?' she asked one morning when the two women lingered over a second cup of coffee.

Nicole looked up. 'Talk about what?'

The words came out easily. But, to Nicole's horror, she felt tears rise in her eyes. Her mother watched her for a moment, then cleared her throat.

'Daddy and I want you to know we're glad you're home, dear.' She patted Nicole's hand and smiled. 'There's a stack of boxes in the attic that have been waiting for me since the day we moved here. If I tackle them on my own, I'll never toss anything away.'

Nicole wiped her eyes and smiled in return. 'I . . . I'm glad to be here, Mama.'

Mae grinned. 'You may end up regretting that statement. I intend to work your tail off.'

Nicole smiled now as she remembered her mother's teasing threat. Work, as her clever mother had certainly known, had been just what she'd needed. She had no idea what her mother had told her father, but he'd asked no more questions and before long she'd been up to her chin in the dusty boxes.

It was all completely mindless. There was no time for thinking or brooding, only doing. Gradually, as the weeks passed, Nicole began to offer herself cautious congratulations. She was, she told herself, putting the whole ugly episode with Chase Tarrant behind her. She was putting it in perspective. She was . . .

She was kidding herself. Her doubts rose as the boxes dwindled; her little game of denial began to fall apart. There was time to think now, and with thinking came awareness. It was slow, at first, images and memories she'd thought buried stealing upon her with a suddenness that always caught her by surprise.

A tall man with broad shoulders, coming into the bait shop, his features blurred by the sun . . .

Chase, she thought, on the island, with the sun beating

down on his tanned shoulders and his smiling face.

But of course it wasn't.

The sound of the water lapping at the shore behind the little grey house . . .

She remembered how he'd looked at her that day they'd bathed in the blue waters of the lagoon.

'Are you all right, Nicole?' her mother would ask, and Nicole would blink and turn blindly towards her.

'Fine,' she'd say, and she'd smile.

But it was a lie. She wasn't fine at all; as the weeks became months, as the blessed numbness that had protected her began to slip away, it was replaced not by the hatred she longed to feel but by a terrible kind of emptiness.

She awoke in the night, filled with an aching longing that surpassed physical desire.

'Chase,' she'd whisper, when her sleep-fogged brain couldn't censor itself, when the feel of his arms and his mouth were as real as the sound of the wind on the bay.

And, as the dream faded, Nicole would slip into her bathrobe and sit curled beside the window, watching the cold blaze of the night sky, remembering another sky and the heat of a million tiny suns . . .

'Nicole?'

Nicole blinked at the sound of her mother's voice. She looked up in surprise. How long had she been sitting on this bench? she wondered, as she shivered with the cold.

'Nicole.'

She blinked again and focused her eyes. Her mother was standing at the side door of the house, watching her with a concerned expression. Nicole swallowed drily and forced a smile to her lips.

'I . . . I was just trying to get some sun,' she said, rising quickly from the bench. 'It feels lovely, doesn't it?'

'I suppose it must have, before it dipped behind that

cloud—and that was more than half an hour ago,' her mother said drily.

'Now that you mention it,' Nicole said with a self-conscious laugh, 'it is chilly, isn't it? Are you warm enough in that old sweater of Daddy's?'

Her mother looked down at herself and smiled. 'Not exactly *haute couture*, is it?' She tugged at the hem of the sweater and sighed. 'Come keep me company while I make your father some coffee. He's bound and determined to finish varnishing the shelves in the shop this afternoon. He's convinced spring is going to arrive all of a sudden and we'll be overrun with customers.'

Nicole smiled as she followed her mother into the house and sat down at the kitchen table. 'He may be right. I saw a fishing-boat on the bay a little while ago.'

'It's warming up, I admit.' Mae peered into her daughter's face as she filled the coffee-pot. 'At least the sun's put some colour into your cheeks—although you still could use another five pounds.'

'I'm fine, Mama.' Nicole smiled gently. 'Really. I've done nothing but eat and sleep for the past four months. If I'm not careful, I'll turn into a slug.'

Her mother laughed softly. 'I don't think there's any danger of that. Your father's planning on putting you to work once the season starts.'

'It's good of you to say that, Mama, but we both know he doesn't really need me. The two of you can run the shop easily.'

Mae Sorensen shook her head. 'Believe me, Nicole, I can use all the help I can get. I don't know the first thing about fishing-rods and reels, and you know it. As for bait . . .' Her mother shuddered delicately. 'I'd just as soon leave that subject alone.'

'Well, I'm glad to help out.' Nicole looked down at the table. 'But I can't stay here forever,' she said.

Mae Sorensen nodded. 'No, you can't,' she said briskly. 'This is no place for a vital young woman, Nicole—especially when her heart's still in Coral City, Florida.'

'What are you talking about, Mama? Do you mean Aston Powell? I told you, that wasn't serious. I . .'

Her mother's eyes narrowed. 'Don't play games with me, Nicole. You know exactly what I'm talking about.'

Nicole shoved back her chair. 'I don't want any coffee, Mama. I . . .'

'That man,' her mother said flatly, her eyes on her daughter's face. 'You never did tell us his name.'

'Mama, please, I don't know wh . . .'

'The one you were with on that island. The one who saved your life.'

'This is silly, Mama. Whatever brought this on? I . . .'

'Nicole.' Her mother's voice was sharp. 'Why do you cry in your sleep?'

Nicole rose. 'I refuse to discuss this. You have no right . . .'

'I have every right. I love you.'

'That doesn't permit you to be unkind.'

The older woman caught hold of her shoulders. 'Not half as unkind as hearing you cry in the middle of the night, or seeing the terrible sadness in your face when you think no one's watching.'

'Stop it, please. There's no point.'

'Of course there's a point! How long do you think the three of us can go on pretending everything is just fine and dandy, Nicole?' Mae slipped into a chair and looked at her daughter. 'Your father lies awake half the night, worrying about you, wondering what happened . . .'

'Nothing happened,' Nicole said. 'Can't you just . . .?'

'One moment you were living in Florida, happy with

your new life, and the next thing we knew you were here, looking as if you'd lost your best friend.'

Nicole sank into her seat again. Was it her imagination, or were there new lines beside her mother's mouth? Caught up in her own grief, had she been blind to the pain she'd inflicted on others?

She took a breath. 'I'm just . . . it's just that . . .' Her voice trembled. 'I'm so ashamed, Mama,' she whispered.

Her mother's hand covered hers. 'Of what, dear? There's never anything shameful about loving someone.' She looked into her daughter's eyes. 'I was right, wasn't I? You're running from that man you were shipwrecked with.'

Nicole shook her head. 'No. I'm not running from him. He—he doesn't care if I'm—if I'm . . .' Her eyes locked with her mother's. 'He's just like Tony,' she whispered. 'Exactly like Tony. They say lightning doesn't strike twice, but it does, Mama.' Tears rolled down her cheeks. 'I made the same stupid mistake again.'

'No.' Her mother's voice was firm. 'I may not know all the details, but I do know it's not at all the same as what happened between you and Tony.'

Nicole's lips trembled. 'You're right, it's not. I should be grateful to Chase Tarrant for that much. It took me a long time to see through Tony. At least, with Chase, it was quick.'

Her mother smiled. 'Do you realise that's the first time you've mentioned his name?' she asked softly.

Nicole sighed. 'I'm sorry if I've been a mope,' she said, forcing a smile to her lips. 'But . . .'

'A mope?' Mae Sorensen laughed. 'Nicole,' she said gently, 'I remember when you and Tony separated—I went to stay with you in Chicago for a few weeks. I saw how you wandered around that big apartment of yours, looking like a whipped puppy.'

'I was terribly upset. I . . .'

'Nicole.' Her mother's fingers laced through hers. 'Tony was your husband. You lived with him for three years. But I never heard you sobbing your heart out the way you do for this—this Chase person. I never saw you look as if you'd lost everything.'

Nicole tugged her hand free of her mother's. 'I don't want to discuss this any more,' she said in an unsteady voice. 'You don't know . . .'

Her mother nodded. 'You're right. The only thing I *do* know is what my instincts tell me—you still love this man.'

'No, I do not. I'm just . . . my pride's hurt, that's all. I . . .'

'I don't believe you,' her mother said flatly.

Nicole's eyes filled with angry tears. 'Dammit, Mama! He doesn't love me, don't you understand? He . . . he used me, to . . . to . . .'

The older woman squeezed her hand. 'To what?' she prompted gently.

Nicole shook her head. 'It's much too complicated to explain,' she said wearily. 'He used me to get even. He—he boasted about it. And then he—then he accused me of having used him . . .'

Mae's eyebrows rose. 'Which is it?'

'What do you mean?'

Her mother shrugged. 'I just don't see how he could accuse you and use you at the same time, Nicole. Did you ask him to explain that?'

Nicole stared at her. 'You're talking in riddles, Mama.'

Mae smiled. 'I have the feeling you and your Mr Tarrant didn't talk at all.'

'Believe me, Chase Tarrant and I are all talked out.'

'People who love each other are never talked out,

Nicole. How do you think your father and I agreed to move to this place? We talked about how much he wanted this kind of life, how much I'd enjoy the Peninsula Music Fest each summer at Ephraim . . .'

'It's not the same thing at all, Mama.' Nicole pushed her chair away from the table and got to her feet. 'Please,' she said wearily, 'let's just drop it, all right? I'm going to lie down for a while before dinner. Unless you need me to help with something . . .'

Her mother sighed. 'No,' she said finally, 'no, nothing. You go on and lie down, dear. I'll call you when dinner's ready.'

Nicole kissed her mother's cheek as she went by. 'Thanks, Mama.'

Her mother sighed again. 'For what, dear? I haven't done anything—I just wish I could. That's been the worst of all this—your father and I both feel so useless.'

Nicole smiled as she started towards her room. 'You've done a lot. And I'm grateful.'

Her smile faded as she closed the door to her room. Her mother's 'shock treatment' had stunned her, but maybe it was long overdue. Maybe you had to face the truth before you could start over. Maybe . . .

She reached into her pocket and her fingers brushed against the pocket-knife Chase had given her. It had been a gift of hatred, but it was all she had of him, and she couldn't part with it.

Tears glistened on her lashes. 'Oh, God,' she whispered, 'how can I still love him?'

It was a terrible question, one she'd spent the long winter pondering. But there was no point denying it any longer. She loved Chase, she would always love him. He'd probably forgotten about her by now, but she would always remember everything about him: the ever-changing grey of his eyes, the warmth of his kisses, the feel of him in her arms.

A ship's horn sounded its mournful cry far out in the bay. Somewhere deep in the house, the telephone echoed a shrill response. Nicole put the back of her hand to her mouth. How impossible it all was—her mother on the phone, her father whistling as he slapped varnish on the bait shop's worn shelves—the sounds of life were all around her and she was dying, inch by slow inch, dying for a lost love, for a love that had never really been.

'Nicole. Nicole, darling, could you do me a favour, please?'

She rubbed her hands across her eyes and took a steadying breath. 'Yes,' she whispered, and then she swallowed hard and opened her bedroom door. 'Yes, Mama,' she called. 'What is it?'

Her mother stepped into the hallway, her eyes gleaming with excitement. 'You'll never believe it,' she said happily. 'That was your father on the phone. We have a customer!'

Nicole wiped her eyes and laughed. 'That's not exactly the event of the year, is it? Anyway, who'd be silly enough to want to fish on such a day?'

Mae shrugged her shoulders. ' "Ours not to reason why," ' she laughed.

Nicole sighed. 'And Daddy's hands are full of varnish.' She shrugged into her quilted jacket as she started towards the door. 'All right, I'll go to the shop and take care of it.'

Her mother gave a strange little laugh. 'No,' she said. 'He's not at the store. He rented a boat—it's at the marina.' She touched her tongue to her lips. 'You can run over to slip fourteen with some sandwiches, can't you, darling?'

Nicole looked at her mother in surprise. 'Deliver

them, you mean? Well, sure, I suppose I can.'

'Good. I knew you'd do it.' She reached up and stroked Nicole's hair. 'Nicole . . .'

Nicole frowned. 'Mama,' she said, 'what on earth is wrong with you? You seem so—I don't know—so funny.'

Mae Sorensen's smile trembled, then vanished. 'I . . . I just want you to remember that I wouldn't do this if I didn't think it was the right thing to do, darling,' she said softly. 'Sometimes, fate deals us cards we have to play.' Her eyes searched her daughter's face. 'Do you understand?'

Nicole sighed. 'Honestly, Mama, I don't mind. I mean, ordinarily, I'd tell some hotshot who wanted delivery service to come and get his stuff himself. But, seeing as he wants one of your sandwiches . . .' She smiled and kissed her mother's cheek. 'I know how important this is.'

Her mother nodded. 'You can't imagine,' she said softly.

CHAPTER TWELVE

THE SKY had turned gunmetal-grey when Nicole left the house. The colour gave the water an ominous cast. The wind had picked up, too, and it almost stole her breath as she hurried along the narrow walk that led to the marina. She made a face, shifted the package she held, and pulled up the hood of her coat.

'Who is this fool who wants his lunch hand-delivered?' she'd grumbled to her mother.

'Now, Nicole, that's no way to talk about a customer. And he didn't ask for delivery—your father suggested it. He thought it was easier than giving him directions to the shop.'

'Directions?' Nicole had laughed. 'Go two blocks, make a left turn . . .'

'He's not from around here, Nicole. The marina gave him our number.'

Nicole had sighed as she closed the buttons on her coat. 'Stop worrying, Mama. I'll be polite. But the man's still a fool to take a boat out on a day like this.'

Now, as she walked through the all but deserted marina, she revised her opinion. He was worse than that. He had to be stupid to want to risk Sturgeon Bay with a storm obviously blowing in from across the lake. 'Ours not to reason why,' her mother had said. Well, that was true enough, but she would at least offer a warning along with the sandwiches. If he still insisted on going out after that—Nicole gave a mental shrug. She'd have done her part.

Most of the slips were empty. The boats that normally moored within them had been dry-docked for the season. A few hardy fishermen had their boats in the water already, trying for the big one that had got away last summer.

Nicole's footsteps slowed, then stopped. Slip fourteen. Wasn't that what her mother had said? But that had to be a mistake. The boat moored at slip fourteen was no fishing-craft. It was a powerboat, long, lean and menacing. It sat among the other boats like a wolf tethered among sheep.

The wind whipped the hood back from her face. Nicole took a step forward, trying to ignore the sudden rapid tattoo of her heart. The last time she'd seen a boat like this was the day she'd met Chase. It was different—the shiny hull was burgundy instead of black—but its purpose was the same.

It was a boat that spoke of speed and aggression, of a man who would laugh in the face of danger and turn his face to the wind . . .

Her breath hissed as she drew it into her lungs. What was the matter with her? Was she going to go through life as if she'd been hypnotised, then left with an image that would trigger a response months later?

She'd spent only a handful of days with Chase, but she couldn't seem to set them aside. Her marriage had lasted years; when it was over, the pain had lingered, but the heart-wrenching memories of love had fled. Why couldn't the same thing happen now? Why did she have to keep remembering?

The wind ruffled her hair and she pulled up her hood as she walked up the dock to the slip. The powerboat jerked at the end of its line, as if it were waiting to break free. She could see no one on board or on the dock nearby. Perhaps whoever owned her was in the cabin.

She cleared her throat. 'Hello?'

Her voice sounded faint over the increasing moan of the wind. She swallowed and put her hands to her mouth.

'Hello!' she called again. 'Is there anybody on board?'

There was only silence. Nicole shrugged irritably. What could you expect from someone who owned a boat such as this, someone who was determined to take it out on this kind of day?

She had two choices. Take the sandwiches back home or leave them on board, and to hell with the protocol that said you never boarded a boat without permission. Well, she wasn't about to leave them—they hadn't been paid for yet. And if she took the damned things back her mother would probably accuse her of not having been polite or some such nonsense. There was another choice, of course. She could stand around in the cold, waiting for the boat's owner. But she damned well wasn't going to do that.

A note. She'd leave a note, explaining that she'd brought the food, as promised, and that if the bloody fool who'd ordered it still wanted it, he could pick it up at the shop.

She stepped carefully on to the deck, balancing herself as the hull dipped lightly beneath her weight. The boat was beautiful—it was all leather, wood and gleaming high-tech plastic. Chase's boat had been like that, she remembered; it had a kind of savage grace that had reminded her of him . . .

She shook her head irritably as she dug into her shoulder-bag. She was getting worse, not better, acting as if she were a love-struck schoolgirl instead of a woman who'd been twice burned.

Dammit! There wasn't a pen or a pencil in her bag, not even a lipstick stub. Her eyes flew to the cabin. The hatch was open. She'd gone this far—why not a little further? There was sure to be some kind of writing material below.

She scrambled down the companionway ladder. The cabin was dark and cool. She thought, for a moment, there was a familiar scent in the air—something masculine that brought with it a rush of memories . . .

'Stop it,' she whispered aloud. 'Just find a pen or a pencil and a piece of paper.'

There was both pen and paper on the navigation desk. She touched the tip of her tongue to her lips, then bent over the desk.

'Dear sir, she scrawled, 'the sandwiches you ordered . . .'

Footsteps thudded on deck. Nicole's heart thudded, too. The pen fell from her fingers and she looked up. The owner was back; it was time to announce herself and clamber up the steps.

She took a step towards the companionway. Her tongue felt too large for her mouth, and her palms were suddenly damp. What was the matter with her? All she had to do was call out and explain who she was.

You're acting like a fool, Nicole, she thought wildly. I know what you're afraid of, and you're crazy. He'll turn out to be short and fat and bald, he'll pull out his wallet to pay you for the sandwiches and a dozen pictures of his kids will fall out in one of those accordion-pleated plastic things . . . She swallowed and moved another step. For goodness sake, she told herself, it won't be Chase. You're never going to see him again . . .

The engines roared to life. She gasped and lurched backwards as the boat moved away from the dock, slowly at first, then faster. The packet of sandwiches fell from her hands and she grasped the railing alongside the ladder and climbed to the deck.

'Hey,' she yelled, 'wait a minute! You've made a mistake. I was below, writing you a note, and . . .'

No! Her words caught in her throat, then tumbled

away. The man at the wheel turned towards her. Something blazed to life in his eyes, then was snuffed out by a look of such ruthlessness that she felt the chill of it in the marrow of her bones.

It was Chase.

'What are you doing here?' His voice was low, but it carried clearly over the deep roar of the engines.

'What am I . . .?' She pushed a tangle of dark hair back from her face and swallowed drily. 'I think I'm the one who should be asking that question.'

She cried out as his hand closed on her shoulder. 'Answer me, Nicole. What are you doing here?'

His eyes were as dark as the sky that hung over them. She swallowed again and willed her racing heart to slow before it exploded.

'I was delivering the sandwiches you ordered,' she said carefully. 'You owe me four dollars and twenty-fi . . .'

'I see. You're in the catering business now, is that it?'

She lifted her chin. 'My parents own the shop you telephoned, Captain Tarrant.'

'Your parents.' His voice was flat. 'Sorensen's Bait and Tackle Shop is owned by your parents?'

'Yes. My mother asked me to . . .'

Chase's mouth twisted. 'Wheeler isn't your maiden name, then.'

Nicole shook her head. 'No. It was my husband's name. I . . .' She drew a breath. 'What business is it of yours, anyway?'

His hand bit through the quilted coat and into her flesh. 'I should have guessed as much. Hell, nothing you told me about yourself was true.'

'Everything I told you was true.'

His eyes narrowed. 'Nicole Wheeler, you said. From Dayton, Illinois, you said.'

'Yes, that's right.'

Chase shook his head. 'Nicole Sorensen, of the Wisconsin Sorensens. That's who you are, Miss Wheeler.'

'So what? You just turn this boat around and take me back.'

'Nobody ever heard of you in Dayton, Nicole. And they never heard of your piano-teacher mother or your father who owns a haberdashery.'

Disbelief registered in her eyes. 'What are you talking about? My mother never taught piano in Dayton—she taught it years ago, before she and Daddy married. And he never owned a haberdashery. He was a salesman for a company that made men's accessories; he travelled through the mid-west until he and Mama retired here . . .' She fell silent. 'Were you . . . were you in Dayton, asking about my family?'

'Yes. No.' His voice roughened. 'I was asking about you, dammit. And no one had ever heard of you.' His mouth turned downwards. 'But I wasn't surprised. You'd told me so many damned lies as it was . . .'

'I never lied to you, Chase. I . . .' Her voice trembled, then broke. 'Why were you looking for me?' she whispered. He said nothing, and she drew in her breath, then let it out slowly. 'I don't believe it! Weren't you satisfied? You did enough to me. You . . .'

'No,' he snarled, 'I was not satisfied. I'm *still* not satisfied.' She flinched as he grasped her shoulder and shook her. 'I want answers, damn you. And until I get them . . .'

Nicole felt a flutter of fear. 'Take me back to shore. Right now, Chase. Take me . . .'

His lips drew away from his teeth. 'With pleasure,' he said in a silken whisper. 'Right after you tell me what I want to know.'

'Chase, listen to me. There's a storm coming up. You don't know how treacherous these waters can be.'

His eyes gleamed darkly. 'Ah, sweet Nicole, I know all about treachery. Have you forgotten?'

'No,' she whispered, remembering what he'd done to her, 'no, I . . . I remember. But the weather . . .'

Chase laughed, just as he had that day the storm had swept towards *Enchantress.* 'I've been searching for you for four months. You don't really think a little storm warning is going to stop me now?'

Her pulse tripped. No, she thought, watching his face, no, she knew him too well to think that. Nothing would stop him from getting whatever it was he wanted, and heaven only knew what that might be. There had always been a kind of restrained violence about him; now, it was an unseen presence between them. Hadn't he humiliated her enough that terrible night in Charlotte Amalie? Had he wanted more, had he wanted to shame her in Coral City, too?

She looked into his eyes, and the blazing anger she saw in them made terror leap to her throat.

'Take me back to shore,' she demanded.

Chase laughed. His hand fell away from her and he took the wheel. 'We've played this scene before, Nicole.'

'Take me back, Chase. My parents know I made a delivery to slip fourteen. They can find out whose boat was moored there.'

He laughed again. 'That won't take any great effort. I gave my name to the woman who took my order.'

Nicole's breath caught. 'My mother?' she asked in an incredulous whisper. 'You told her who you were?'

He looked at her as if she were crazy. 'It's the way you usually place an order, isn't it?'

The phone had rung not ten minutes after she and her mother had talked. 'You never mentioned his name before,' Mae Sorensen had said, and then the phone had rung, she'd picked it up, and a man's voice had said, 'This is Chase Tarrant.'

Nicole closed her eyes. All those strange apologies her
mother had offered made sense now. Mae Sorensen, who
believed in love and in the power of talking things out, had
grasped at what she thought was a chance to ease her
daughter's broken heart.

If only I'd told you the whole story, Mama . . .

Nicole's eyes flew open. The powerboat was at full
throttle, racing like a thoroughbred horse across the greasy
water ahead to where the sky and the water came together
in a cold, pewter-coloured haze.

'Did you hear me, Chase Tarrant?' Nicole's voice rose
over the snarling engines. 'You are to take me . . .' She
cried out as he locked the wheel and lifted her into his
arms. 'What do you think you're doing?' she yelled.
'Chase! Put me down!'

It was as if time were running backwards. All of this had
happened before: Chase, carrying her to the companionway, then tossing her over his shoulder and taking her
below. Chase, dumping her on to a bunk, then standing
over her with his hands on his hips and a cold, dangerous
look on his face.

'Don't move,' he said softly. 'Don't touch anything. Do
you understand?'

'Damn you,' Nicole whispered. 'You can't . . .'

His teeth flashed. 'Just watch me.'

She watched in disbelief as he ripped the microphone
from the radio and tossed it aside, then turned and
climbed the companionway ladder to the deck. The hatch
cover slammed closed, and the grey half-light of the
approaching storm closed around her.

She drew a steadying breath and then another, but it
seemed hard to get enough air into her lungs. It was
foolish to be so frightened, she told herself. What could he
possibly do to her? He had been angry with her before,

yes, but even when things had been at their worst he'd never hurt her.

And yet, there was a savagery about him she had never seen before. And there was a recklessness, too, one that terrified her. He knew there was a storm warning, yet he was sailing right into the teeth of it. The Chase Tarrant she'd sailed with had faced danger willingly, but to go looking for it was quite different.

Nicole started as the engines fell silent. The hatch opened; daylight as thick and colourless as lead filled the cabin and then was obliterated by Chase's shadow. He came down the ladder slowly, pausing at the bottom.

'All right,' he said in a grim, quiet voice, 'no one's going to disturb us now.'

She rose slowly. Her hands were trembling and she shoved them deep into her pockets before he could notice.

'Chase, listen to me. I don't know what you want from me. I . . .'

'Why didn't you go back to Coral City?'

Her lips felt dry. She ran her tongue across them, then swallowed. 'I did. I caught a flight in the morning . . .'

He shook his head. 'I went to your apartment. Your landlord said you'd moved out that afternoon.'

Nicole nodded. 'Yes, that's right. I told him . . .'

'You told him nothing. No forwarding address, no telephone number, no nothing.'

She nodded again. 'I wasn't sure where I was going. I just got into my car and drove.'

His lips became a thin line. 'Why didn't Powell want you any more? Was it because he knew you and I had slept together?'

The blunt question sent a flood of colour to her cheeks. 'What are you talking about?'

Chase shrugged. 'It was pretty simple to figure out. The plan only called for you to sabotage *Enchantress,* nothing else.' His eyes darkened. 'When he realised you'd slept with me, he told you to get out.'

Nicole stared into his face and then she turned her back to him. 'I'm not going to let you do this to me,' she said in a trembling whisper. 'You've done enough to last me a lifetime. You . . .'

His fingers bit into her shoulders and he whirled her towards him. 'Why?' The word was a rasping whisper. 'Why did you do it, Nicole? Did you sleep with me because you thought it would hurt me to find out you really belonged to Powell?'

'I never "belonged" to anybody. And I won't . . .'

'Or did you get carried away by the moonlight and the warm breeze? Was I just part of some tropical fantasy?'

Tears of rage rose in Nicole's eyes. 'Damn you to hell, Chase Tarrant,' she whispered. 'I wish I'd never set eyes on you.'

He gave a short, bitter laugh. '*You* wish, Nicole? That's what I've wished every day and night for the past four months. I wished it while I looked through the Chicago suburbs, searching for a man named Wheeler who owned a men's clothing store, while I drove around Lake Winnebago, while I drove from one end of Sturgeon Bay to another . . .'

'Why? What do you want from me, Chase?' Nicole's voice broke. 'You've already taken everything—there's nothing left.'

His hands tightened. 'The truth, damn you! That's what I want.'

She hadn't the strength to fight him any more. She knew what he wanted: his ego needed salvaging, he wanted to hear her say she'd gone into his arms because she couldn't resist him. If only he knew how true that was, she thought, and her eyes filled with tears again.

'I wish I'd thrown those damned sandwiches into the

bay,' she said brokenly. 'I wish I'd never boarded this boat . . .'

He looked at her. 'Why did you?'

She laughed through her tears. 'I didn't want to lose a customer for my father. When I didn't see anyone on board, I decided to write a note.'

Chase's face turned white. 'A note,' he breathed. 'Another goddamned note. You're good at that, aren't you?'

Nicole stared at him. 'What are you talking about?'

'This,' he snarled, pushing her from him. He dug into his pocket and pulled out a folded slip of white paper. 'Here,' he said, shoving it into her hands, 'read it, in case you've forgotten. I know it by heart.'

Her hands shook as she took the worn piece of paper from him and smoothed it open.

'Dear Aston, I haven't much time to write this. Chase Tarrant's in for a shock. Someone had to teach him a lesson, a lesson he'll remember as long as he lives, and I wanted to be that someone.'

She looked at her name, scrawled beneath the words she'd written to Aston the night she'd decided to sneak on board *Enchantress* and sabotage her, a lifetime ago in Coral City.

'No,' she said softly, 'I haven't forgotten this note. I'm not proud of it, but . . .'

Chase caught hold of her. 'What a sap I was, Nicole! There you were, trying to get even with me for what you thought I'd done to your boyfriend, and all the time, all the time . . .'

'I was wrong to have done that, Chase. I admitted it to you. I said I was sorry . . .'

His hands slid along her arms to her wrists. '. . . all the time, I was falling in love with you. When I think of it now—I was like a schoolboy.'

Nicole looked at him in stunned silence. 'You . . . you were falling in love with me?' she whispered.

'And you were so convincing. When I held you in my arms that last day on the island . . .' His eyes blazed into hers, his face a pale mask in the darkening cabin. 'I'd never dreamed I could love a woman as I love you.' His voice fell to a whisper. 'And I never will again.'

Nicole's heart leaped. Chase loved her, he'd said. He would always love her. But it couldn't be—he'd said such terrible things to her, he'd humiliated her . . .

'That day we were rescued, I came to your suite to tell you how much you meant to me. I'd meant to tell you on the island, but everything happened too quickly.'

Tears of joy filled her eyes. 'Chase,' she whispered.

'I was going to ask you to marry me, Nicole. I'd run the scene over in my mind a dozen times.'

She drew in her breath. 'And you found Aston in my suite.'

His mouth narrowed. 'Yes. Powell, with that smug look on his face. Powell, telling me I'd been had . . . I didn't want to believe him. And then he whipped out that note. I'll never forget how he smiled when he handed it to me. "I hope you have a sense of humour, Tarrant," he said.'

Nicole looked at him blankly. 'Why would he have done that? That note was written . . .'

'He said it explained your behaviour better than he ever could. He said you'd left it at the yacht club desk for him after our rescue. He said . . .'

Nicole's eyes widened. Everything was beginning to fall into place. 'No. That's not true, Chase. Aston lied.'

He drew her towards him roughly. 'Dammit, there's no point in playing games now. I know you wrote that note. I saw you, remember? I didn't think of it until Powell mentioned it. I saw you handing the desk clerk an envelope when I came into the clubhouse.'

For the first time in months, Nicole felt a tiny flame of hope flicker in her breast.

'Chase,' she said, her eyes on his, 'the note Aston showed you, the one you just showed me—I wrote it the night I decided to stow away on *Enchantress*.'

Chase's eyes narrowed warily. 'Don't play games, I said.'

A wry smile touched her lips. 'The note you saw me hand the desk clerk said I didn't want to see Aston until I'd bathed and rested.'

Far out in Lake Michigan, a boat horn sounded. The cry was a sorrowful one, as if it had been torn from a broken heart. Chase stared into Nicole's eyes.

'I'd have thought you'd have been eager to see Powell,' he said slowly. 'It had been over a week.'

'I wasn't at all eager,' she said softly. 'I didn't look forward to telling him I'd fallen in love with you.'

Silence stretched between them, broken only by the soft lap of the water against the hull.

'Say that again,' Chase murmered.

Her lips curved in a smile. 'I love you Chase. You're all I've thought about all these lonely months.'

He whispered her name and drew her into his arms. Nicole closed her eyes as she nestled against him. Suddenly, she felt his muscles tense and he clasped her shoulders and held her from him.

'That son of a bitch,' he growled. 'He deliberately showed me the wrong note.'

She nodded. 'Yes. It all makes sense now. That's why he opened his shirt and took off his tie, to make it look as if he and I . . .' She looked into Chase's eyes. 'Aston came to my suite unannounced. I thought it was you—I was so happy that I opened the door without asking any questions. I told Aston I loved you and he got angry, but then he begged me to let him make it up to the both of us. I went into the bedroom to dress, and then I thought better of it. I came out to tell him it was a bad idea.'

'And I was there,' Chase said with a groan, 'all set up to leap at the bait like a trout rising to a fly.' His arms closed around her and he gathered her to him. 'Nicole, my love,' he whispered, 'can you ever forgive me?'

She smiled as she leaned back in his arms and looked up at him. 'There's nothing to forgive,' she said. 'We've both been terribly foolish—and I still feel somehow responsible for *Enchantress*. I know how much she meant to you, how much winning that race meant . . .'

Chase laughed softly. 'Do you still have that pocket-knife I gave you?'

Her eyebrows rose. 'Yes,' she said slowly, 'I've carried it with me all these months.' She put her hand into her pocket and pulled the knife out. 'Here it is. But . . .'

He took her by the hand and led her on deck. To her surprise, she saw that they were anchored in a quiet cove not far from the marina. The storm clouds that had threatened a short while ago had moved off, leaving the sky awash in the magenta and violet colours that came with sunset.

'Give me the knife,' Chase said.

She handed it to him, watching as he ran his thumb lightly along the worn handle. Then he smiled, drew back his arm, and hurled the knife far out over the water. It arced through the air and fell into the bay.

'Chase! That knife was important to you. It . . .'

His arms closed around her. 'I've won the only thing that matters,' he whispered.

And when he kissed her, Nicole knew it was true.

Harlequin Presents

Coming Next Month

Available in March wherever paperback books are sold, or through
Harlequin Reader Service:

In the U.S.	In Canada
901 Fuhrmann Blvd.	P.O. Box 603
P.O. Box 1397	Fort Erie, Ontario
Buffalo, N.Y 14240-1397	L2A 5X3

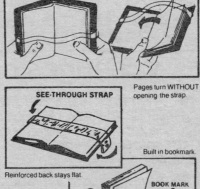

February brings you . . .

Harlequin Presents...

Award of Excellence

PENNY JORDAN

valentine's night

Sorrel didn't particularly want to meet her long-lost cousin Val from Australia. However, since the girl had come all this way just to make contact, it seemed a little churlish not to welcome her.

As there was no room at home, it was agreed that Sorrel and Val would share the Welsh farmhouse that was being renovated for Sorrel's brother and his wife. Conditions were a bit primitive, but that didn't matter.

At least, not until Sorrel found herself snowed in with the long-lost cousin, who turned out to be a handsome, six-foot male!

Also, look for the next Harlequin Presents Award of Excellence title in April:

Elusive as the Unicorn
by Carole Mortimer

HP1243-1